George Meredith

Selected Poems of George Meredith

George Meredith

Selected Poems of George Meredith

ISBN/EAN: 9783744766517

Printed in Europe, USA, Canada, Australia, Japan

Cover: Foto ©Andreas Hilbeck / pixelio.de

More available books at **www.hansebooks.com**

SELECTED POEMS

BY

GEORGE MEREDITH

WESTMINSTER

ARCHIBALD CONSTABLE AND CO.

2 WHITEHALL GARDENS

1897

CONTENTS

CONTENTS

*The selection here made has
been under the supervision of
the Author*

WOODLAND PEACE

Sweet as Eden is the air,
  And Eden-sweet the ray.
No Paradise is lost for them
Who foot by branching root and stem,
And lightly with the woodland share
  The change of night and day.

Here all say,
We serve her, even as I :
We brood, we strive to sky,
We gaze upon decay,
We wot of life through death,
How each feeds each we spy;
And is a tangle round,
Are patient ; what is dumb,
We question not, nor ask
The silent to give sound,
The hidden to unmask,
The distant to draw near.

A

And this the woodland saith :
I know not hope or fear ;
I take whate'er may come ;
I raise my head to aspects fair,
From foul I turn away.

Sweet as Eden is the air.
    And Eden-sweet the ray.

THE LARK ASCENDING

He rises and begins to round,
He drops the silver chain of sound,
Of many links without a break,
In chirrup, whistle, slur and shake,
All intervolved and spreading wide,
Like water-dimples down a tide
Where ripple ripple overcurls
And eddy into eddy whirls;
A press of hurried notes that run
So fleet they scarce are more than one,
Yet changeingly the trills repeat
And linger ringing while they fleet,
Sweet to the quick o' the ear, and dear
To her beyond the handmaid ear,
Who sits beside our inner springs,
Too often dry for this he brings,

Which seems the very jet of earth
At sight of sun, her music's mirth,
As up he wings the spiral stair,
A song of light, and pierces air
With fountain ardour, fountain play,
To reach the shining tops of day,
And drink in everything discerned
An ecstasy to music turned,
Impelled by what his happy bill
Disperses ; drinking, showering still,
Unthinking save that he may give
His voice the outlet, there to live
Renewed in endless notes of glee,
So thirsty of his voice is he,
For all to hear and all to know
That he is joy, awake, aglow ;
The tumult of the heart to hear
Through pureness filtered crystal-clear,
And know the pleasure sprinkled bright
By simple singing of delight ;
Shrill, irreflective, unrestrained,
Rapt, ringing, on the jet sustained
Without a break, without a fall,
Sweet-silvery, sheer lyrical,

Perennial, quavering up the chord
Like myriad dews of sunny sward
That trembling into fulness shine,
And sparkle dropping argentine ;
Such wooing as the ear receives
From zephyr caught in choric leaves
Of aspens when their chattering net
Is flushed to white with shivers wet ;
And such the water-spirit's chime
On mountain heights in morning's prime,
Too freshly sweet to seem excess,
Too animate to need a stress ;
But wider over many heads
The starry voice ascending spreads,
Awakening, as it waxes thin,
The best in us to him akin ;
And every face to watch him raised,
Puts on the light of children praised ;
So rich our human pleasure ripes
When sweetness on sincereness pipes,
Though nought be promised from the seas,
But only a soft-ruffling breeze
Sweep glittering on a still content,
Serenity in ravishment

For singing till his heaven fills,
'Tis love of earth that he instils,
And ever winging up and up,
Our valley is his golden cup,
And he the wine which overflows
To lift us with him as he goes:
The woods and brooks, the sheep and kine,
He is, the hills, the human line,
The meadows green, the fallows brown,
The dreams of labour in the town;
He sings the sap, the quickened veins;
The wedding song of sun and rains
He is, the dance of children, thanks
Of sowers, shout of primrose-banks,
And eye of violets while they breathe;
All these the circling song will wreathe,
And you shall hear the herb and tree,
The better heart of men shall see,
Shall feel celestially, as long
As you crave nothing save the song.

Was never voice of ours could say
Our inmost in the sweetest way,

Like yonder voice aloft, and link
All hearers in the song they drink.
Our wisdom speaks from failing blood,
Our passion is too full in flood,
We want the key of his wild note
Of truthful in a tuneful throat ;
The song seraphically free
Of taint of personality,
So pure that it salutes the suns
The voice of one for millions,
In whom the millions rejoice
For giving their one spirit voice.   .
Yet men have we, whom we revere,
Now names, and men still housing here,
Whose lives, by many a battle-dint
Defaced, and grinding wheels on flint,
Yield substance, though they sing not, sweet
For song our highest heaven to greet :
Whom heavenly singing gives us new,
Enspheres them brilliant in our blue,
From firmest base to farthest leap,
Because their love of Earth is deep,
And they are warriors in accord
With life to serve, and pass reward,

So touching purest and so heard
In the brain's reflex of yon bird :
Wherefore their soul in me, or mine,
Through self-forgetfulness divine,
In them, that song aloft maintains,
To fill the sky and thrill the plains
With showerings drawn from human stores,
As he to silence nearer soars,
Extends the world at wings and dome,
More spacious making more our home,
Till lost on his aërial rings
In light, and then the fancy sings.

THE ORCHARD AND THE HEATH

I CHANCED upon an early walk to spy
A troop of children through an orchard gate :
    The boughs hung low, the grass was high ;
    They had but to lift hands or wait
For fruits to fill them ; fruits were all their sky.

They shouted, running on from tree to tree,
And played the game the wind plays, on and round.
    'Twas visible invisible glee
    Pursuing ; and a fountain's sound
Of laughter spouted, pattering fresh on me.

I could have watched them till the daylight fled,
Their pretty bower made such a light of day.
    A small one tumbling sang, 'Oh ! head !'
    The rest to comfort her straightway
Seized on a branch and thumped down apples red.

The tiny creature flashing through green grass,
And laughing with her feet and eyes among
    Fresh apples, while a little lass
    Over as o'er breeze-ripples hung :
That sight I saw, and passed as aliens pass.

My footpath left the pleasant farms and lanes,
Soft cottage-smoke, straight cocks a-crow, gay
        flowers ;
    Beyond the wheel-ruts of the wains,
    Across a heath I walked for hours,
And met its rival tenants, rays and rains.

Still in my view mile-distant firs appeared,
When, under a patched channel-bank enriched
    With foxglove whose late bells drooped seared,
    Behold, a family had pitched
Their camp, and labouring the low tent upreared.

Here, too, were many children, quick to scan
A new thing coming ; swarthy cheeks, white teeth :
    In many-coloured rags they ran,
    Like iron runlets of the heath.
Dispersed lay broth-pot, sticks, and drinking-can.

Three girls, with shoulders like a boat at sea
Tipped sideways by the wave (their clothing slid
 From either ridge unequally),
 Lean, swift and voluble, bestrid
A starting-point, unfrocked to the bent knee.

They raced; their brothers yelled them on, and
   broke
In act to follow, but as one they snuffed
 Wood-fumes, and by the fire that spoke
 Of provender, its pale flame puffed,
And rolled athwart dwarf furzes grey-blue smoke.

Soon on the dark edge of a ruddier gleam,
The mother-pot perusing, all, stretched flat,
 Paused for its bubbling-up supreme :
 A dog upright in circle sat,
And oft his nose went with the flying steam.

I turned and looked on heaven awhile, where now
The moor-faced sunset broadened with red light ;
 Threw high aloft a golden bough,
 And seemed the desert of the night
Far down with mellow orchards to endow.

SEED-TIME

I

FLOWERS of the willow-herb are wool ;
Flowers of the briar berries red ;
Speeding their seed as the breeze may rule,
Flowers of the thistle loosen the thread.
Flowers of the clematis drip in beard,
Slack from the fir-tree youngly climbed ;
Chaplets in air, flies foliage seared ;
Heeled upon earth, lie clusters rimed.

II

Where were skies of the mantle stained
Orange and scarlet, a coat of frieze
Travels from North till day has waned,
Tattered, soaked in the ditch's dyes ;
Tumbles the rook under grey or slate ;
Else enfolding us, damps to the bone ;
Narrows the world to my neighbour's gate ;
Paints me Life as a wheezy crone.

III

Now seems none but the spider lord;
Star in circle his web waits prey,
Silvering bush-mounds, blue brushing sward :
Slow runs the hour, swift flits the ray.
Now to his thread-shroud is he nigh,
Nigh to the tangle where wings are sealed,
He who frolicked the jewelled fly ;
All is adroop on the down and the weald.

IV

Mists more lone for the sheep-bell enwrap
Nights that tardily let slip a morn
Paler than moons, and on noontide's lap
Flame dies cold, like the rose late born.
Rose born late, born withered in bud !—
I, even I, for a zenith of sun
Cry, to fulfil me, nourish my blood :
O for a day of the long light, one !

V

Master the blood, nor read by chills,
Earth admonishes : Hast thou ploughed,

Sown, reaped, harvested grain for the mills,
Thou hast the light over shadow of cloud.
Steadily eyeing, before that wail
Animal-infant, thy mind began,
Momently nearer me : should sight fail,
Plod in the track of the husbandman.

VI

Verily now is our season of seed,
Now in our Autumn ; and Earth discerns
Them that have served her in them that can
    read,
Glassing, where under the surface she burns,
Quick at her wheel, while the fuel, decay,
Brightens the fire of renewal : and we ?
Death is the word of a bovine day,
Know you the breast of the springing To-be.

OUTER AND INNER

I

FROM twig to twig the spider weaves
  At noon his webbing fine.
So near to mute the zephyrs flute
  That only leaflets dance.
The sun draws out of hazel leaves
  A smell of woodland wine.
I wake a swarm to sudden storm
  At any step's advance.

II

Along my path is bugloss blue,
  The star with fruit in moss;
The foxgloves drop from throat to top
  A daily lesser bell.
The blackest shadow, nurse of dew,
  Has orange skeins across;
And keenly red is one thin thread
  That flashing seems to swell.

15.

III

My world I note ere fancy comes,
  Minutest hushed observe;
What busy bits of motioned wits
  Through antlered mosswork strive.
But now so low the stillness hums,
  My springs of seeing swerve,
For half a wink to thrill and think
  The woods with nymphs alive.

IV

I neighbour the invisible
  So close that my consent
Is only asked for spirits masked
  To leap from trees and flowers.
And this because with them I dwell
  In thought, while calmly bent
To read the lines dear Earth designs
  Shall speak her life on ours.

V

Accept, she says; it is not hard
  In woods; but she in towns

Repeats, accept; and have we wept,
   And have we quailed with fears,
Or shrunk with horrors, sure reward
   We have whom knowledge crowns;
Who see in mould the rose unfold,
   The soul through blood and tears.

WIND ON THE LYRE

THAT was the chirp of Ariel
You heard, as overhead it flew,
The farther going more to dwell,
And wing our green to wed our blue ;
But whether note of joy or knell,
Not his own Father-singer knew ;
Nor yet can any mortal tell,
Save only how it shivers through ;
The breast of us a sounded shell,
The blood of us a lighted dew.

DIRGE IN WOODS

A wind sways the pines,
        And below
Not a breath of wild air;
Still as the mosses that glow
On the flooring and over the lines
Of the roots here and there.
The pine-tree drops its dead;
They are quiet, as under the sea.
Overhead, overhead
Rushes life in a race,
'As the clouds the clouds chase;
        And we go,
And we drop like the fruits of the tree,
        Even we,
        Even so.

CHANGE IN RECURRENCE

I

I stood at the gate of the cot
Where my darling, with side-glance demure,
Would spy, on her trim garden-plot,
The busy wild things chase and lure.
For these with their ways were her feast;
They had surety no enemy lurked.
Their deftest of tricks to their least,
She gathered in watch as she worked.

II

When berries were red on her ash.
The blackbird would rifle them rough,
Till the ground underneath looked a gash,
And her rogue grew the round of a chough.

20

The squirrel cocked ear o'er his hoop,
Up the spruce, quick as eye, trailing brush.
She knew any tit of the troop
All as well as the snail-tapping thrush.

III

I gazed : 'twas the scene of the frame,
With the face, the dear life for me, fled.
No window a lute to my name,
No watcher there plying the thread.
But the blackbird hung pecking at will ;
The squirrel from cone hopped to cone ;
The thrush had a snail in his bill,
And tap-tapped the shell hard on a stone.

HARD WEATHER

Bursts from a rending East in flaws
The young green leaflet's harrier, sworn
To strew the garden, strip the shaws,
And show our Spring with banner torn.
Was ever such virago morn?
The wind has teeth, the wind has claws.
All the wind's wolves through woods are loose,
The wild wind's falconry aloft.
Shrill underfoot the grassblade shrews,
At gallop, clumped, and down the croft
Bestrid by shadows, beaten, tossed:
It seems a scythe, it seems a rod.
The howl is up at the howl's accost;
The shivers greet and the shivers nod.

Is the land ship? we are rolled, we drive
Tritonly, cleaving hiss and hum;
Whirl with the dead, or mount or dive,
Or down in dregs, or on in scum.

And drums the distant, pipes the near,
And vale and hill are grey in grey,
As when the surge is crumbling sheer,
And sea-mews wing the haze of spray.
Clouds—are they bony witches?—swarms,
Darting swift on the robber's flight,
Hurry an infant sky in arms :
It peeps, it becks; 'tis day, 'tis night.
Black while over the loop of blue
The swathe is closed, like shroud on corse.
Lo, as if swift the Furies flew,
The Fates at heel at a cry to horse .

Interpret me the savage whirr :
And is it Nature scourged, or she,
Her offspring's executioner,
Reducing land to barren sea ?
But is there meaning in a day
When this fierce angel of the air,
Intent to throw, and haply slay,
Can for what breath of life we bear,
Exact the wrestle ?—Call to mind
The many meanings glistening up

When Nature to her nurslings kind,
Hands them the fruitage and the cup !
And seek we rich significance
Not otherwhere than with those tides
Of pleasure on the sunned expanse,
Whose flow deludes, whose ebb derides ?

Look in the face of men who fare
Lock-mouthed, a match in lungs and thews
For this fierce angel of the air,
To twist with him and take his bruise.
That is the face beloved of old
Of Earth, young mother of her brood :
Nor broken for us shows the mould
When muscle is in mind renewed :
Though farther from her nature rude,
Yet nearer to her spirit's hold :
And though of gentler mood serene,
Still forceful of her fountain-jet.
So shall her blows be shrewdly met,
Be luminously read the scene
Where Life is at her grindstone set,
That she may give us edgeing keen,

String us for battle, till as play
The common strokes of fortune shower.
Such meaning in a dagger-day
Our wits may clasp to wax in power.
Yea, feel us warmer at her breast,
By spin of blood in lusty drill,
Than when her honeyed hands caressed,
And Pleasure, sapping, seemed to fill.

Behold the life at ease; it drifts.
The sharpened life commands its course.
She winnows, winnows roughly; sifts,
To dip her chosen in her source:
Contention is the vital force,
Whence pluck they brain, her prize of gifts,
Sky of the senses! on which height,
Not disconnected, yet released,
They see how spirit comes to light,
Through conquest of the inner beast,
Which Measure tames to movement sane,
In harmony with what is fair.
Never is Earth misread by brain :
That is the welling of her, there

The mirror : with one step beyond,
For likewise is it voice ; and more,
Benignest kinship bids respond,
When wail the weak, and them restore
Whom days as fell as this may rive,
While Earth sits ebon in her gloom,
Us atomies of life alive
Unheeding, bent on life to come.
Her children of the labouring brain,
These are the champions of the race,
True parents, and the sole humane,
With understanding for their base.
Earth yields the milk, but all her mind
Is vowed to thresh for stouter stock.
Her passion for old giantkind,
That scaled the mount, uphurled the rock,
Devolves on them who read aright
Her meaning and devoutly serve ;
Nor in her starlessness of night
Peruse her with the craven nerve
But even as she from grass to corn,
To eagle high from grubbing mole,
Prove in strong brain her noblest born,
The station for the flight of soul.

THE SOUTH-WESTER

DAY of the cloud in fleets! O day
Of wedded white and blue, that sail
Immingled, with a footing ray
In shadow-sandals down our vale !—
And swift to ravish golden meads,
Swift up the run of turf it speeds,
Thy bright of head and dark of heel,
To where the hilltop flings on sky,
As hawk from wrist or dust from wheel,
The tiptoe scalers tossed to fly :—
Thee the last thunder's caverned peal
Delivered from a wailful night :
All dusky round thy cradled light,
Those brine-born issues, now in bloom
Transfigured, wreathed as raven's plume
And briony-leaf to watch thee lie :
Dark eyebrows o'er a dreamful eye

Nigh opening : till in the braid
Of purpled vapours thou wert rosed .
Till that new babe a Goddess maid
Appeared and vividly disclosed
Her beat of life : then crimson played
On edges of the plume and leaf :
Shape had they and fair feature brief,
The wings, the smiles : they flew the breast,
Earth's milk.   But what imperial march
Their standards led for earth, none guessed
Ere upward of a coloured arch,
An arrow straining eager head
Lightened, and high for zenith sped.
Fierier followed ; followed Fire.
Name the young lord of Earth's desire,
Whose look her wine is, and whose mouth
Her music !   Beauteous was she seen
Beneath her midway West of South ;
And sister was her quivered green
To sapphire of the Nereid eyes
On sea when sun is breeze ; she winked
As they, and waved, heaved waterwise
Her flood of leaves and grasses linked :
A myriad lustrous butterflies

A moment in the fluttering sheen;
Becapped with the slate air that throws
The reindeer's antlers black between
Low-frowning and wide-fallen snows,
A minute after; hooded, stoled
To suit a graveside Season's dirge.
Lo, but the breaking of a surge,
And she is in her lover's fold,
Illumined o'er a boundless range
Anew: and through quick morning hours
The Tropic-Arctic counterchange
Did seem to pant in beams and showers.

But noon beheld a larger heaven;
Beheld on our reflecting field
The Sower to the Bearer given,
And both their inner sweetest yield,
Fresh as when dews were grey or first
Received the flush of hues athirst.
Heard we the woodland, eyeing sun,
As harp and harper were they one.
A murky cloud a fair pursued,
Assailed, and felt the limbs elude:

He sat him down to pipe his woe,
And some strange beast of sky became :
A giant's club withheld the blow ;
A milky cloud went all to flame.
And there were groups where silvery springs
The ethereal forest showed begirt
By companies in choric rings,
Whom but to see made ear alert.
For music did each movement rouse,
And motion was a minstrel's rage
To have our spirits out of house,
And bathe them on the open page.
This was a day that knew not age.
Since flew the vapoury twos and threes
From western pile to eastern rack ;
As on from peaks of Pyrenees
To Graians ; youngness ruled the track.
When songful beams were shut in caves,
And rainy drapery swept across ;
When the ranked clouds were downy waves,
Breast of swan, eagle, albatross,
In ordered lines to screen the blue,
Youngest of light was nigh, we knew.
The silver finger of it laughed

Along the narrow rift : it shot,
Slew the huge gloom with golden shaft,
Then haled on high the volumed blot,
To build the hurling palace, cleave
The dazzling chasm ; the flying nests,
The many glory-garlands weave,
Whose presence not our sight attests
Till wonder with the splendour blent,
And passion for the beauty flown,
Make evanescence permanent,
The thing at heart our endless own.

Only at gathered eve knew we
The marvels of the day : for then
Mount upon mountain out of sea
Arose, and to our spacious ken
Trebled sublime Olympus round
In towering amphitheatre.
Colossal on enormous mound,
Majestic gods we saw confer.
They wafted the Dream-messenger
From off the loftiest, the crowned :
That Lady of the hues of foam
In sun-rays : who, close under dome,

A figure on the foot's descent,
Irradiate to vapour went,
As one whose mission was resigned,
Dispieced, undraped, dissolved to threads;
Melting she passed into the mind,
Where immortal with mortal weds.

Whereby was known that we had viewed
The union of our earth and skies
Renewed : nor less alive renewed
Than when old bards, in nature wise,
Conceived pure beauty given to eyes,
And with undyingness imbued.
Pageant of man's poetic brain,
His grand procession of the song,
It was ; the Muses and their train ;
Their God to lead the glittering throng :
At whiles a beat of forest gong ;
At whiles a glimpse of Python slain.
Mostly divinest harmony,
The lyre, the dance.   We could believe
A life in orb and brook and tree
And cloud ; and still holds Memory
A morning in the eyes of eve.

THE THRUSH IN FEBRUARY

I know him, February's thrush,
And loud at eve he valentines
On sprays that paw the naked bush
Where soon will sprout the thorns and bines.

Now ere the foreign singer thrills
Our vale his plain-song pipe he pours,
A herald of the million bills;
And heed him not, the loss is yours.

My study, flanked with ivied fir
And budded beech with dry leaves curled,
Perched over yew and juniper,
He neighbours, piping to his world :—

C

The wooded pathways dank on brown,
The branches on grey cloud a web,
The long green roller of the down,
An image of the deluge-ebb :—

And farther, they may hear along
The stream beneath the poplar row.
By fits, like welling rocks, the song
Spouts of a blushful Spring in flow.

But most he loves to front the vale
When waves of warm South-western rains
Have left our heavens clear in pale,
With faintest beck of moist red veins .

Vermilion wings, by distance held
To pause aflight while fleeting swift :
And high aloft the pearl inshelled
Her lucid glow in glow will lift ;

A little south of coloured sky ;
Directing, gravely amorous,
The human of a tender eye
Through pure celestial on us :

Remote, not alien; still, not cold;
Unraying yet, more pearl than star;
She seems a while the vale to hold
In trance, and homelier makes the far.

Then Earth her sweet unscented breathes,
An orb of lustre quits the height;
And like blue iris-flags, in wreaths
The sky takes darkness, long ere quite.

His Island voice then shall you hear,
Nor ever after separate
From such a twilight of the year
Advancing to the vernal gate.

He sings me, out of Winter's throat,
The young time with the life ahead;
And my young time his leaping note
Recalls to spirit-mirth from dead.

Imbedded in a land of greed,
Of mammon-quakings dire as Earth's,
My care was but to soothe my need;
At peace among the littleworths.

To light and song my yearning aimed;
To that deep breast of song and light
Which men have barrenest proclaimed;
As 'tis to senses pricked with fright.

So mine are these new fruitings rich
The simple to the common brings;
I keep the youth of souls who pitch
Their joy in this old heart of things:

Who feel the Coming young as aye,
Thrice hopeful on the ground we plough;
Alive for life, awake to die;
One voice to cheer the seedling Now.

Full lasting is the song, though he,
The singer, passes: lasting too,
For souls not lent in usury,
The rapture of the forward view.

With that I bear my senses fraught
Till what I am fast shoreward drives.
They are the vessel of the Thought.
The vessel splits, the Thought survives.

Nought else are we when sailing brave,
Save husks to raise and bid it burn.
Glimpse of its livingness will wave
A light the senses can discern

Across the river of the death,
Their close.   Meanwhile, O twilight bird
Of promise! bird of happy breath!
I hear, I would the City heard.

The City of the smoky fray;
A prodded ox, it drags and moans:
Its Morrow no man's child; its Day
A vulture's morsel beaked to bones.

It strives without a mark for strife;
It feasts beside a famished host:
The loose restraint of wanton life,
That threatened penance in the ghost!

Yet there our battle urges; there
Spring heroes many: issuing thence,
Names that should leave no vacant air
For fresh delight in confidence.

Life was to them the bag of grain,
And Death the weedy harrow's tooth.
Those warriors of the sighting brain
Give worn Humanity new youth.

Our song and star are they to lead
The tidal multitude and blind
From bestial to the higher breed
By fighting souls of love divined.

They scorned the ventral dream of peace,
Unknown in nature.   This they knew:
That life begets with fair increase
Beyond the flesh, if life be true.

Just reason based on valiant blood,
The instinct bred afield woûld match
To pipe thereof a swelling flood,
Were men of Earth made wise in watch.

Though now the numbers count as drops
An urn might bear, they father Time.
She shapes anew her dusty crops;
Her quick in their own likeness climb.

Of their own force do they create;
They climb to light, in her their root.
Your brutish cry at muffled fate
She smites with pangs of worse than brute.

She, judged of shrinking nerves, appears
A Mother whom no cry can melt;
But read her past desires and fears,
The letters on her breast are spelt.

A slayer, yea, as when she pressed
Her savage to the slaughter-heaps,
To sacrifice she prompts her best:
She reaps them as the sower reaps.

But read her thought to speed the race,
And stars rush forth of blackest night:
You chill not at a cold embrace
To come, nor dread a dubious might.

Her double visage, double voice,
In oneness rise to quench the doubt.
This breath, her gift, has only choice
Of service, breathe we in or out.

Since Pain and Pleasure on each hand
Led our wild steps from slimy rock
To yonder sweeps of gardenland,
We breathe but to be sword or block.

The sighting brain her good decree
Accepts; obeys those guides, in faith,
By reason hourly fed, that she,
To some the clod, to some the wraith,

Is more, no mask ; a flame, a stream.
Flame, stream, are we, in mid career
From torrent source, delirious dream,
To heaven-reflecting currents clear.

And why the sons of Strength have been
Her cherished offspring ever; how
The Spirit served by her is seen
Through Law ; perusing love will show.

Love born of knowledge, love that gains
Vitality as Earth it mates,
The meaning of the Pleasures, Pains,
The Life, the Death, illuminates.

For love we Earth, then serve we all;
Her mystic secret then is ours:
We fall, or view our treasures fall,
Unclouded, as beholds her flowers

Earth, from a night of frosty wreck,
Enrobed in morning's mounted fire,
When lowly, with a broken neck,
The crocus lays her cheek to mire.

TARDY SPRING

Now the North wind ceases,
The warm South-west awakes;
Swift fly the fleeces,
Thick the blossom-flakes.

Now hill to hill has made the stride,
And distance waves the without end:
Now in the breast a door flings wide;
Our farthest smiles, our next is friend.
And song of England's rush of flowers
Is this full breeze with mellow stops,
That spins the lark for shine, for showers;
He drinks his hurried flight, and drops.
The stir in memory seem these things,
Which out of moistened turf and clay
Astrain for light push patient rings,
Or leap to find the waterway.

'Tis equal to a wonder done,
Whatever simple lives renew .
Their tricks beneath the father sun,
As though they caught a broken clue;
So hard was earth an eyewink back:
But now the common life has come,
The blotting cloud a dappled pack,
The grasses one vast underhum.
A City clothed in snow and soot,
With lamps for day in ghostly rows,
Breaks to the scene of hosts afoot,
The river that reflective flows:
And there did fog down crypts of street
Play spectre upon eye and mouth:—
Their faces are a glass to greet
This magic of the whirl for South.
A burly joy each creature swells
With sound of its own hungry quest;
Earth has to fill her empty wells,
And speed the service of the nest;
The phantom of the snow-wreath melt,
That haunts the farmer's look abroad,
Who sees what tomb a white night built,
Where flocks now bleat and sprouts the clod.

For iron Winter held her firm;
Across her sky he laid his hand;
And bird he starved, he stiffened worm;
A sightless heaven, a shaven land.
Her shivering Spring feigned fast asleep,
The bitten buds dared not unfold:
We raced on roads and ice to keep
Thought of the girl we love from cold.

But now the North wind ceases,
The warm South-west awakes,
The heavens are out in fleeces,
And earth's green banner shakes.

BREATH OF THE BRIAR

I

O BRIAR-SCENTS, on yon wet wing
Of warm South-west wind brushing by,
You mind me of the sweetest thing
That ever mingled frank and shy:
When she and I, by love enticed,
Beneath the orchard-apples met,
In equal halves a ripe one sliced,
And smelt the juices ere we ate.

II

That apple of the briar-scent,
Among our lost in Britain now,
Was green of rind, and redolent
Of sweetness as a milking cow.
The briar gives it back, well nigh
The damsel with her teeth on it;
Her twinkle between frank and shy,
My thirst to bite where she had bit.

YOUNG REYNARD

I

GRACEFULLEST leaper, the dappled fox-cub
Curves over brambles with berries and buds,
Light as a bubble that flies from the tub,
Whisked by the laundry-wife out of her suds.
Wavy he comes, woolly, all at his ease,
Elegant, fashioned to foot with the deuce;
Nature's own prince of the dance: then he sees
Me, and retires as if making excuse.

II

Never closed minuet courtlier! Soon
Cub-hunting troops were abroad, and a yelp
Told of sure scent: ere the stroke upon noon
Reynard the younger lay far beyond help.
Wild, my poor friend, has the fate to be chased;
Civil will conquer: were t' other 'twere worse,
Fair, by the flushed early morning embraced,
Haply you live a day longer in verse.

46

LOVE IN THE VALLEY

UNDER yonder beech-tree single on the green-
    sward,
  Couched with her arms behind her golden head,
Knees and tresses folded to slip and ripple idly,
  Lies my young love sleeping in the shade.
Had I the heart to slide an arm beneath her,
  Press her parting lips as her waist I gather slow,
Waking in amazement she could not but embrace
    me :
  Then would she hold me and never let me go?

*

*   *

Shy as the squirrel and wayward as the swallow,
  Swift as the swallow along the river's light
Circleting the surface to meet his mirrored winglets,
  Fleeter she seems in her stay than in her flight.

47

Shy as the squirrel that leaps among the pine-tops,
  Wayward as the swallow overhead at set of sun,
She whom I love is hard to catch and conquer,
  Hard, but O the glory of the winning were she
    won !

*

*   *

When her mother tends her before the laughing
    mirror,
  Tying up her laces, looping up her hair,
Often she thinks, were this wild thing wedded,
  More love should I have, and much less care.
When her mother tends her before the lighted
    mirror,
  Loosening her laces, combing down her curls,
Often she thinks, were this wild thing wedded,
  I should miss but one for the many boys and girls.

*

*   *

Heartless she is as the shadow in the meadows
  Flying to the hills on a blue and breezy noon.
No, she is athirst and drinking up her wonder :
  Earth to her is young as the slip of the new moon.

Deals she an unkindness, 'tis but her rapid measure,
  Even as in a dance ; and her smile can heal no
    less :
Like the swinging May-cloud that pelts the flowers
    with hailstones
Off a sunny border, she was made to bruise and
    bless.   .

*

    *   *

Lovely are the curves of the white owl sweeping
  Wavy in the dusk lit by one large star.
Lone on the fir-branch, his rattle-note unvaried,
  Brooding o'er the gloom, spins the brown eve-jar
Darker grows the valley, more and more forgetting .
  So were it with me if forgetting could be willed.
Tell the grassy hollow that holds the bubbling
    well-spring,
  Tell it to forget the source that keeps it filled.

*

    *   *

Stepping down the hill with her fair companions,
  Arm in arm, all against the raying West,
Boldly she sings, to the merry tune she marches,
  Brave in her shape, and sweeter unpossessed.

D

Sweeter, for she is what my heart first awaking
    Whispered the world was; morning light is she.
Love that so desires would fain keep her changeless,
    Fain would fling the net, and fain have her free.

*

*   *

Happy happy time, when the white star hovers
    Low over dim fields fresh with bloomy dew,
Near the face of dawn, that draws athwart the
        darkness,
    Threading it with colour, like yewberries the yew.
Thicker crowd the shades as the grave East deepens
    Glowing, and with crimson a long cloud swells.
Maiden still the morn is; and strange she is, and
        secret;
    Strange her eyes; her cheeks are cold as cold
        sea-shells.

*

*   *

Sunrays, leaning on our southern hills and lighting
    Wild cloud-mountains that drag the hills along,
Oft ends the day of your shifting brilliant laughter
    Chill as a dull face frowning on a song.

Ay, but shows the South-west a ripple-feathered
    bosom
  Blown to silver while the clouds are shaken and
    ascend   '
Scaling the mid-heavens as they stream, there comes
    a sunset
  Rich, deep like love in beauty without end.

*

     * .   *

When at dawn she sighs, and like an infant to the
    window
  Turns grave eyes craving light, released from
    dreams,
Beautiful she looks, like a white water-lily
  Bursting out of bud in havens of the streams.
When from bed she rises clothed from neck to
    ankle
  In her long nightgown sweet as boughs of May,
Beautiful she looks, like a tall garden lily
  Pure from the night, and splendid for the day.

*

     *   *

Mother of the dews, dark eye-lashed twilight,
  Low-lidded twilight, o'er the valley's brim,

Rounding on thy breast sings the dew-delighted
    skylark,
  Clear as though the dewdrops had their voice in
    him.
Hidden where the rose-flush drinks the rayless planet,
  Fountain-full he pours the spraying fountain-
    showers.
Let me hear her laughter, I would have her ever
  Cool as dew in twilight, the lark above the flowers.

*

*   *

All the girls are out with their baskets for the
    primrose ;
  Up lanes, woods through, they troop in joyful
    bands.
My sweet leads: she knows not why, but now she
    loiters,
  Eyes bent anemones, and hangs her hands.
Such a look will tell that the violets are peeping,
  Coming the rose : and unaware a cry
Springs in her bosom for odours and for colour,
  Covert and the nightingale ; she knows not why.

*

*   *

Kerchiefed head and chin, she darts between her
 tulips,
Streaming like a willow grey in arrowy rain :
Some bend beaten cheek to gravel, and their
 angel
She will be ; she lifts them, and on she speeds
 again.
Black the driving raincloud breasts the iron gate-
 way :
She is forth to cheer a neighbour lacking mirth.
So when sky and grass met rolling dumb for
 thunder,
Saw I once a white dove, sole light of earth.

*

* *

Prim little scholars are the flowers of her garden,
 Trained to stand in rows, and asking if they
 please.
I might love them well but for loving more the wild
 ones.
O my wild ones ! they tell me more than these.
You, my wild one, you tell of honied field-rose,
 Violet, blushing eglantine in life ; and even as
 they,

They by the wayside are earnest of your goodness,
   You are of life's, on the banks that line the way.

           *

   *   *

Peering at her chamber the white crowns the red
      rose,
   Jasmine winds the porch with stars two and three.
Parted is the window; she sleeps; the starry
      jasmine
   Breathes a falling breath that carries thoughts of
      me.
Sweeter unpossessed, have I said of her my sweetest?
   Not while she sleeps: while she sleeps the
      jasmine breathes,
Luring her to love; she sleeps; the starry jasmine
   Bears me to her pillow under white rose-wreaths.

           *

   *   *

Yellow with birdfoot-trefoil are the grass-glades;
   Yellow with cinquefoil of the dew-grey leaf:
Yellow with stonecrop; the moss-mounds are yellow;
   Blue-necked the wheat sways, yellowing to the
      sheaf.

Green-yellow, bursts from the copse the laughing
    yaffle;
  Sharp as a sickle is the edge of shade and shine:
Earth in her heart laughs looking at the heavens,
    Thinking of the harvest: I look and think of
    mine.

        *

  *   *

This I may know: her dressing and undressing
  Such a change of light shows as when the skies
    in sport
Shift from cloud to moonlight; or edging over
    thunder
  Slips a ray of sun; or sweeping into port
White sails furl; or on the ocean borders
  White sails lean along the waves leaping green.
Visions of her shower before me, but from eyesight
  Guarded she would be like the sun were she seen.

        *

  *   *

Front door and back of the mossed old farmhouse
  Open with the morn, and in a breezy link
Freshly sparkles garden to stripe-shadowed orchard,
  Green across a rill where on sand the minnows
  wink.

Busy in the grass the early sun of summer
  Swarms, and the blackbird's mellow fluting notes
Call my darling up with round and roguish chal-
    lenge :
  Quaintest, richest carol of all the singing throats !

             *

    *   *

Cool was the woodside ; cool as her white dairy
  Keeping sweet the cream-pan; and there the
    boys from school,
Cricketing below, rushed brown and red with sun-
    shine ;
  O the dark translucence of the deep-eyed cool !
Spying from the farm, herself she fetched a pitcher
  Full of milk, and tilted for each in turn the beak.
Then a little fellow, mouth up and on tiptoe,
  Said, 'I will kiss you': she laughed and leaned
    her cheek.

             *

    *   *

Doves of the fir-wood walling high our red roof
  Through the long noon coo, crooning through
    the coo.

Loose droop the leaves, and down the sleepy road-
way
  Sometimes pipes a chaffinch; loose droops the
blue.
Cows flap a slow tail knee-deep in the river,
  Breathless, given up to sun and gnat and fly.
Nowhere is she seen; and if I see her nowhere,
  Lightning may come, straight rains and tiger sky.

*
     *   *

O the golden sheaf, the rustling treasure-armful
  O the nutbrown tresses nodding interlaced!
O the treasure-tresses one another over
  Nodding! O the girdle slack about the waist!
Slain are the poppies that shot their random scarlet
  Quick amid the wheatears: wound about the
waist,
Gathered, see these brides of earth one blush of
ripeness!
  O the nutbrown tresses nodding interlaced!

*
     *   *

Large and smoky red the sun's cold disk drops,
  Clipped by naked hills, on violet shaded snow:

Eastward large and still lights up a bower of moon-
    rise,
    Whence at her leisure steps the moon aglow.
Nightlong on black print-branches our beech-tree
    Gazes in this whiteness: nightlong could I.
Here may life on death or death on life be painted.
    Let me clasp her soul to know she cannot die!

*
*   *

Gossips count her faults; they scour a narrow
    chamber
    Where there is no window, read not heaven or
        her.
'When she was a tiny,' one aged woman quavers,
    Plucks at my heart and leads me by the ear.
Faults she had once as she learnt to run and
    tumbled:
    Faults of feature some see, beauty not complete.
Yet, good gossips, beauty that makes holy
    Earth and air, may have faults from head to feet.

*
*   *

Hither she comes; she comes to me; she lingers,
    Deepens her brown eyebrows, while in new sur-
        prise

High rise the lashes in wonder of a stranger;
  Yet am I the light and living of her eyes.
Something friends have told her fills her heart to
    brimming,
  Nets her in her blushes, and wounds her, and
    tames.—
Sure of her haven, O like a dove alighting,
  Arms up, she dropped: our souls were in our names.
          *
  *   *

Soon will she lie like a white-frost sunrise.
  Yellow oats and brown wheat, barley pale as rye,
Long since your sheaves have yielded to the
    thresher,
  Felt the girdle loosened, seen the tresses fly.
Soon will she lie like a blood-red sunset.
  Swift with the to-morrow, green-winged Spring!
Sing from the South-west, bring her back the
    truants,
  Nightingale and swallow, song and dipping wing.
          *
  *   *

Soft new beech-leaves, up to beamy April
  Spreading bough on bough a primrose mountain,
    you

Lucid in the moon, raise lilies to the skyfields,
  Youngest green transfused in silver shining
    through:
Fairer than the lily, than the wild white cherry:
  Fair as in image my seraph love appears
Borne to me by dreams when dawn is at my eye-
    lids:
  Fair as in the flesh she swims to me on tears.

*

*   *

Could I find a place to be alone with heaven,
  I would speak my heart out: heaven is my need.
Every woodland tree is flushing like the dogwood,
  Flashing like the whitebeam, swaying like the
    reed.
Flushing like the dogwood crimson in October;
  Streaming like the flag-reed South-west blown;
Flashing as in gusts the sudden-lighted whitebeam:
  All seem to know what is for heaven alone.

MARIAN

I

SHE can be as wise as we,
    And wiser when she wishes;
She can knit with cunning wit,
    And dress the homely dishes.
She can flourish staff or pen,
    And deal a wound that lingers
She can talk the talk of men,
    And touch with thrilling fingers.

II

Match her ye across the sea,
    Natures fond and fiery;
Ye who zest the turtle's nest
    With the eagle's eyrie.
Soft and loving is her soul,
    Swift and lofty soaring;
Mixing with its dove-like dole
    Passionate adoring.

                                         a

III

Such a she who 'll match with me?
    In flying or pursuing,
Subtle wiles are in her smiles
    To set the world a-wooing.
She is steadfast as a star,
    And yet the maddest maiden:
She can wage a gallant war,
    And give the peace of Eden.

HYMN TO COLOUR

I

WITH Life and Death I walked when Love appeared,
And made them on each side a shadow seem.
Through wooded vales the land of dawn we neared,
Where down smooth rapids whirls the helmless
    dream
To fall on daylight; and night puts away
            Her darker veil for grey.

II

In that grey veil green grassblades brushed we by;
We came where woods breathed sharp, and over-
    head
Rocks raised clear horns on a transforming sky:
Around, save for those shapes, with him who led
And linked them, desert varied by no sign
            Of other life than mine.

III

By this the dark-winged planet, raying wide,
From the mild pearl-glow to the rose upborne,
Drew in his fires, less faint than far descried,
Pure-fronted on a stronger wave of morn :
And those two shapes the splendour interweaved,
     Hung web-like, sank and heaved.

IV

Love took my hand when hidden stood the sun
To fling his robe on shoulder-heights of snow.
Then said : There lie they, Life and Death in one.
Whichever is, the other is : but know,
It is thy craving self that thou dost see,
     Not in them seeing me.

V

Shall man into the mystery of breath,
From his quick beating pulse a pathway spy ?
Or learn the secret of the shrouded death,
By lifting up the lid of a white eye ?
Cleave thou thy way with fathering desire
     Of fire to reach to fire.

VI

Look now where Colour, the soul's bridegroom,
  makes
The house of heaven splendid for the bride.
To him as leaps a fountain she awakes,
In knotting arms, yet boundless : him beside,
She holds the flower to heaven, and by his power
  Brings heaven to the flower.

VII

He gives her homeliness in desert air,
And sovereignty in spaciousness ; he leads
Through widening chambers of surprise to where
Throbs rapture near an end that aye recedes,
Because his touch is infinite and lends
  A yonder to all ends.

VIII

Death begs of Life his blush ; Life Death persuades
To keep long day with his caresses graced.
He is the heart of light, the wing of shades,
The crown of beauty : never soul embraced
Of him can harbour unfaith ; soul of him
  Possessed walks never dim.

E

IX

Love eyed his rosy memories : he sang:
O bloom of dawn, breathed up from the gold sheaf
Held springing beneath Orient! that dost hang
The space of dewdrops running over leaf;
Thy fleetingness is bigger in the ghost
         Than Time with all his host!

X

Of thee to say behold, has said adieu :
But love remembers how the sky was green,
And how the grasses glimmered lightest blue ;
How saint-like grey took fervour : how the screen
Of cloud grew violet; how thy moment came
         Between a blush and flame.

XI

Love saw the emissary eglantine
Break wave round thy white feet above the gloom ;
Lay finger on thy star; thy raiment line
With cherub wing and limb; wed thy soft bloom,
Gold-quivering like sunrays in thistle-down,
         Earth under rolling brown.

XII

They do not look through love to look on thee,
Grave heavenliness ! nor know they joy of sight,
Who deem the wave of rapt desire must be
Its wrecking and last issue of delight.
Dead seasons quicken in one petal-spot
   Of colour unforgot.

XIII

This way have men come out of brutishness
To spell the letters of the sky and read
A reflex upon earth else meaningless.
With thee, O fount of the Untimed ! to lead,
Drink they of thee, thee eyeing, they unaged
   Shall on through brave wars waged.

XIV

More gardens will they win than any lost;
The vile plucked out of them, the unlovely slain.
Not forfeiting the beast with which they are crossed,
To stature of the Gods will they attain.
They shall uplift their Earth to meet her Lord,
   Themselves the attuning chord !

XV

The song had ceased ; my vision with the song.
Then of those Shadows, which one made descent
Beside me I knew not: but Life ere long
Came on me in the public ways and bent
Eyes deeper than of old : Death met I too,
   And saw the dawn glow through.

MOTHER TO BABE

I

FLECK of sky you are,
Dropped through branches daik,
  O my little one, mine!
Promise of the star,
Outpour of the lark,
  Beam and song divine.

II

See this precious gift,
Steeping in new birth
  All my being, for sign
Earth to heaven can lift,
Heaven descend on earth,
  Both in one be mine!

79

III

Life in light you glass
When you peep and coo,
  You, my little one, mine!
Brooklet chirps to grass,
Daisy looks in dew
  Up to dear sunshine.

NIGHT OF FROST IN MAY

WITH splendour of a silver day,
A frosted night had opened May:
And on that plumed and armoured night,
As one close temple hove our wood,
Its border leafage virgin white.
Remote down air an owl hallooed.
The black twig dropped without a twirl;
The bud in jewelled grasp was nipped;
The brown leaf cracked a scorching curl;
A crystal off the green leaf slipped.
Across the tracks of rimy tan,
Some busy thread at whiles would shoot;
A limping minnow-rillet ran,
To hang upon an icy foot.

In this shrill hush of quietude,
The ear conceived a severing cry.
Almost it let the sound elude,
When chuckles three, a warble shy,

From hazels of the garden came,
Near by the crimson-windowed farm.
They laid the trance on breath and frame,
A prelude of the passion-charm.

Then soon was heard, not sooner heard
Than answered, doubled, trebled, more,
Voice of an Eden in the bird
Renewing with his pipe of four
The sob: a troubled Eden, rich
In throb of heart: unnumbered throats
Flung upward at a fountain's pitch,
The fervour of the four long notes,
That on the fountain's pool subside,
Exult and ruffle and upspring:
Endless the crossing multiplied
Of silver and of golden string.
There chimed a bubbled underbrew
With witch-wild spray of vocal dew.

It seemed a single harper swept
Our wild wood's inner chords and waked
A spirit that for yearning ached
Ere men desired and joyed or wept.

Or now a legion ravishing
Musician rivals did unite
In love of sweetness high to sing
The subtle song that rivals light;
From breast of earth to breast of sky:
And they were secret, they were nigh:
A hand the magic might disperse;
The magic swung my universe.

Yet sharpened breath forbade to dream,
Where all was visionary gleam;
Where Seasons, as with cymbals, clashed;
And feelings, passing joy and woe,
Churned, gurgled, spouted, interflashed,
Nor either was the one we know:
Nor pregnant of the heart contained
In us were they, that griefless plained,
That plaining soared; and through the heart
Struck to one note the wide apart:—
A passion surgent from despair;
A paining bliss in fervid cold;
Off the last vital edge of air,
Leap heavenward of the lofty-souled,

For rapture of a wine of tears;
As had a star among the spheres
Caught up our earth to some mid-height
Of double life to ear and sight,
She giving voice to thought that shines
Keen-brilliant of her deepest mines;
While steely drips the rillet clinked,
And hoar with crust the cowslip swelled.

Then was the lyre of earth beheld,
Then heard by me: it holds me linked;
Across the years to dead-ebb shores
I stand on, my blood-thrill restores.
But would I conjure into me
Those issue notes, I must review
What serious breath the woodland drew;
The low throb of expectancy;
How the white mother-muteness pressed
On leaf and meadow-herb; how shook,
Nigh speech of mouth, the sparkle-crest
Seen spinning on the bracken-crook.

WHIMPER OF SYMPATHY

Hawk or shrike has done this deed
Of downy feathers : rueful sight !
Sweet sentimentalist, invite
Your bosom's Power to intercede.

So hard it seems that one must bleed
Because another needs will bite !
All round we find cold Nature slight
The feelings of the totter-knee'd.

O it were pleasant, with you
To fly from this tussle of foes,
The shambles, the charnel, the wrinkle !
To dwell in yon dribble of dew
On the cheek of your sovereign rose,
And live the young life of a twinkle.

A BALLAD OF PAST MERIDIAN

I

LAST night returning from my twilight walk
I met the grey mist Death, whose eyeless brow
Was bent on me, and from his hand of chalk
He reached me flowers as from a withered bough:
O Death, what bitter nosegays givest thou!

II

Death said, I gather, and pursued his way.
Another stood by me, a shape in stone,
Sword-hacked and iron-stained, with breasts of clay,
And metal veins that sometimes fiery shone:
O Life, how naked and how hard when known!

III

Life said, As thou hast carved me, such am I.
Then memory, like the nightjar on the pine,
And sightless hope, a woodlark in night sky,
Joined notes of Death and Life till night's decline
Of Death, of Life, those inwound notes are mine.

PHOEBUS WITH ADMETUS

I

WHEN by Zeus relenting the mandate was revoked,
    Sentencing to exile the bright Sun-God,
Mindful were the ploughmen of who the steer had
        yoked,
    Who : and what a track showed the upturned sod !
Mindful were the shepherds, as now the noon severe
    Bent a burning eyebrow to brown evetide,
How the rustic flute drew the silver to the sphere,
    Sister of his own, till her rays fell wide.
          God ! of whom music
          And song and blood are pure,
          The day is never darkened
          That had thee here obscure.

II

Chirping none, the scarlet cicadas crouched in ranks :
    Slack the thistle-head piled its down-silk grey :

Scarce the stony lizard sucked hollows in his flanks
    Thick on spots of umbrage our drowsed flocks lay
Sudden bowed the chestnuts beneath a wind unheard
    Lengthened ran the grasses, the sky grew slate :
Then amid a swift flight of winged seed white as curd,
    Clear of limb a Youth smote the master's gate.
            God ! of whom music
            And song and blood are pure,
            The day is never darkened
            That had thee here obscure.

III

Water, first of singers, o'er rocky mount and mead,
    First of earthly singers, the sun-loved rill,
Sang of him, and flooded the ripples on the reed,
    Seeking whom to waken and what ear fill.
Water, sweetest soother to kiss a wound and cool,
    Sweetest and divinest, the sky-born brook,
Chuckled, with a whimper, and made a mirror-pool
    Round the guest we welcomed, the strange hand
        shook.
            God ! of whom music
            And song and blood are pure,
            The day is never darkened
            That had thee here obscure.

IV

Many swarms of wild bees descended on our fields:
    Stately stood the wheatstalk with head bent
        high:
Big of heart we laboured at storing mighty yields,
    Wool and corn, and clusters to make men cry!
Hand-like rushed the vintage; we strung the bellied
        skins
    Plump, and at the sealing the Youth's voice rose:
Maidens clung in circle, on little fists their chins;
    Gentle beasties through pushed a cold long nose.
        God! of whom music
        And song and blood are pure,
        The day is never darkened
        That had thee here obscure.

V

Foot to fire in snowtime we trimmed the slender
        shaft:
    Often down the pit spied the lean wolf's teeth
Grin against his will, trapped by masterstrokes of
        craft;
    Helpless in his froth-wrath as green logs seethe!

Safe the tender lambs tugged the teats, and winter
    sped
Whirled before the crocus, the year's new gold.
Hung the hooky beak up aloft, the arrowhead
    Reddened through his feathers for our dear
      fold.

          God ! of whom music
          And song and blood are pure,
          The day is never darkened
          That had thee here obscure.

VI

Tales we drank of giants at war with Gods above :
    Rocks were they to look on, and earth climbed
      air !
Tales of search for simples, and those who sought
    of love
Ease because the creature was all too fair.
Pleasant ran our thinking that while our work was
    good,
    Sure as fruits for sweat would the praise come
      fast.

He that wrestled stoutest and tamed the billow-
    brood
  Danced in rings with girls, like a sail-flapped mast.
      God! of whom music
      And song and blood are pure,
      The day is never darkened
      That had thee here obscure.

VII

Lo, the herb of healing, when once the herb is
    known,
  Shines in shady woods bright as new-sprung flame.
Ere the string was tightened we heard the mellow
    tone,
  After he had taught how the sweet sounds came.
Stretched about his feet, labour done, 'twas as you
    see
  Red pomegranates tumble and burst hard rind.
So began contention to give delight and be
  Excellent in things aimed to make life kind.
      God! of whom music
      And song and blood are pure,
      The day is never darkened
      That had thee here obscure.

F

VIII

You with shelly horns, rams! and, promontory
  goats,
 You whose browsing beards dip in coldest dew!
Bulls, that walk the pastures in kingly-flashing
  coats!
 Laurel, ivy, vine, wreathed for feasts not few!
You that build the shade-roof, and you that court
  the rays,
 You that leap besprinkling the rock stream-rent:
He has been our fellow, the morning of our days!
 Us he chose for housemates, and this way went.
   God! of whom music
   And song and blood are pure,
   The day is never darkened
   That had thee here obscure.

MELAMPUS

I

With love exceeding a simple love of the things
  That glide in grasses and rubble of woody wreck;
Or change their perch on a beat of quivering wings
  From branch to branch, only restful to pipe and
    peck;
Or, bristled, curl at a touch their snouts in a ball;
  Or cast their web between bramble and thorny
    hook;
The good physician Melampus, loving them all,
  Among them walked, as a scholar who reads a
    book.

II

For him the woods were a home and gave him the
    key
  Of knowledge, thirst for their treasures in herbs
    and flowers.

The secrets held by the creatures nearer than we
  To earth he sought, and the link of their life with
    ours :
And where alike we are, unlike where, and the
    veined
  Division, veined parallel, of a blood that flows
In them, in us, from the source by man unattained
  Save marks he well what the mystical woods dis-
    close.

III

And this he deemed might be boon of love to a
    breast
  Embracing tenderly each little motive shape,
The prone, the flitting, who seek their food whither
    best
  Their wits direct, whither best from their foes
    escape.
For closer drawn to our mother's natural milk,
  As babes they learn where her motherly help is
    great :
They know the juice for the honey, juice for the silk,
  And need they medical antidotes, find them
    straight.

IV

Of earth and sun they are wise, they nourish their
 broods,
 Weave, build, hive, burrow and battle, take joy
  and pain
Like swimmers varying billows : never in woods
 Runs white insanity fleeing itself : all sane
The woods revolve : as the tree its shadowing limns
 To some resemblance in motion, the rooted life
Restrains disorder : you hear the primitive hymns
 Of earth in woods issue wild of the web of strife.

V

Now sleeping once on a day of marvellous fire,
 A brood of snakes he had cherished in grave
  regret
That death his people had dealt their dam and their
  sire,
 Through savage dread of them, crept to his neck,
  and set
Their tongues to lick him : the swift affectionate
  tongue
 Of each ran licking the slumberer : then his ears

A forked red tongue tickled shrewdly: sudden
   upsprung,
    He heard a voice piping: Ay, for he has no
     fears!

VI

A bird said that, in the notes of birds, and the
   speech
    Of men, it seemed: and another renewed: He
     moves
To learn and not to pursue, he gathers to teach;
    He feeds his young as do we, and as we love loves.
No fears have I of a man who goes with his head
    To earth, chance looking aloft at us, kind of hand:
I feel to him as to earth of whom we are fed;
    I pipe him much for his good could he understand.

VII

Melampus touched at his ears, laid finger on wrist:
    He was not dreaming, he sensibly felt and heard.
Above, through leaves, where the tree-twigs thick
    intertwist,
    He spied the birds and the bill of the speaking
     bird.

His cushion mosses in shades of various green,
  The lumped, the antlered, he pressed, while the
    sunny snake
Slipped under: draughts he had drunk of clear
    Hippocrene,
  It seemed, and sat with a gift of the Gods awake.

VIII

Divinely thrilled was the man, exultingly full,
  As quick well-waters that come of the heart of
    earth,
Ere yet they dart in a brook are one bubble-pool
  To light and sound, wedding both at the leap of
    birth.
The soul of light vivid shone, a stream within stream;
  The soul of sound from a musical shell outflew;
Where others hear but a hum and see but a beam,
  The tongue and eye of the fountain of life he
    knew.

IX

He knew the Hours: they were round him, laden
    with seed
Of hours bestrewn upon vapour, and one by one

They winged as ripened in fruit the burden decreed
  For each to scatter; they flushed like the buds in
    sun,
Bequeathing seed to successive similar rings,
  Their sisters, bearers to men of what men have
    earned:
He knew them, talked with the yet unreddened;
    the stings,
  The sweets, they warmed at their bosoms divined,
    discerned.

x

Not unsolicited, sought by diligent feet,
  By riddling fingers expanded, oft watched in
    growth
With brooding deep as the noon-ray's quickening
    wheat,
  Ere touch'd, the pendulous flower of the plants
    of sloth,
The plants of rigidness, answered question and
    squeeze,
  Revealing wherefore it bloomed uninviting, bent,
Yet making harmony breathe of life and disease,
  The deeper chord of a wonderful instrument.

XI

So passed he luminous-eyed for earth and the fates
  We arm to bruise or caress us: his ears were
    charged
With tones of love in a whirl of voluble hates,
  With music wrought of distraction his heart
    enlarged.
Celestial-shining, though mortal, singer, though
    mute,
  He drew the Master of harmonies, voiced or stilled,
To seek him ; heard at the silent medicine-root
  A song, beheld in fulfilment the unfulfilled.

XII

Him Phoebus, lending to darkness colour and form
  Of light's excess, many lessons and counsels gave,
Showed Wisdom lord of the human intricate swarm,
  And whence prophetic it looks on the hives that
    rave,
And how acquired, of the zeal of love to acquire,
  And where it stands, in the centre of life a
    sphere ;
And Measure, mood of the lyre, the rapturous lyre,
  He said was Wisdom, and struck him the notes to
    hear.

XIII

Sweet, sweet: 'twas glory of vision, honey, the
    breeze
  In heat, the run of the river on root and stone,
All senses joined, as the sister Pierides
  Are one, uplifting their chorus, the Nine, his
    own.
In stately order, evolved of sound into sight,
  From sight to sound intershifting, the man
    descried
The growths of earth, his adored, like day out of
    night,
  Ascend in song, seeing nature and song allied.

XIV

And there vitality, there, there solely in song,
  Resides, where earth and her uses to men, their
    needs,
·Their forceful cravings, the theme are : there is it
    strong,
  The Master said : and the studious eye that reads,
(Yea, even as earth to the crown of Gods on the
    mount),
  In links divine with the lyrical tongue is bound.

Pursue thy craft: it is music drawn of a fount
　To spring perennial; well-spring is common
　　ground.

xv

Melampus dwelt among men: physician and sage,
　He served them, loving them, healing them;
　　sick or maimed,
Or them that frenzied in some delirious rage
　Outran the measure, his juice of the woods re-
　　claimed.
He played on men, as his master, Phoebus, on
　　strings
Melodious: as the God did he drive and check,
Through love exceeding a simple love of the things
　That glide in grasses and rubble of woody wreck.

THE APPEASEMENT OF DEMETER

I

DEMETER devastated our good land,
In blackness for her daughter snatched below.
Smoke-pillar or loose hillock was the sand,
Where soil had been to clasp warm seed and throw
The wheat, vine, olive, ripe to Summer's ray.
Now whether night advancing, whether day,
Scarce did the baldness show:
The hand of man was a defeated hand.

II

Necessity, the primal goad to growth,
Stood shrunken; Youth and Age appeared as one;
Like Winter Summer; good as labour sloth;
Nor was there answer wherefore beamed the sun,

Or why men drew the breath to carry pain.
High reared the ploughshare, broken lay the wain,
Idly the flax-wheel spun
Unridered: starving lords were wasp and moth.

III

Lean grassblades losing green on their bent flags,
Sang chilly to themselves; lone honey-bees
Pursued the flowers that were not with dry bags;
Sole sound aloud the snap of sapless trees,
More sharp than slingstones on hard breastplates
    hurled.
Back to first chaos tumbled the stopped world,
Careless to lure or please.
A nature of gaunt ribs, an earth of crags.

IV

No smile Demeter cast: the gloom she saw,
Well draped her direful musing; for in gloom,
In thicker gloom, deep down the cavern-maw,
Her sweet had vanished; liker unto whom,
And whose pale place of habitation mute,
She and all seemed where Seasons, pledged for fruit
Anciently, gaped for bloom:
Where hand of man was as a plucked fowl's claw.

V

The wrathful Queen descended on a vale,
That ere the ravished hour for richness heaved.
Iambe, maiden of the merry tale,
Beside her eyed the once red-cheeked, green-leaved.
It looked as if the Deluge had withdrawn.
Pity caught at her throat, her jests were gone.
More than for her who grieved,
She could for this waste home have piped the wail.

VI

Iambe, her dear mountain-rivulet
To waken laughter from cold stones, beheld
A riven wheatfield cracking for the wet,
And seed like infant's teeth, that never swelled,
Apeep up flinty ridges, milkless round.
Teeth of the giants marked she where thin ground
Rocky in spikes rebelled
Against the hand here slack as rotted net.

VII

The valley people up the ashen scoop
She beckoned, aiming hopelessly to win
Her Mistress in compassion of yon group

So pinched and wizened ; with their aged grin,
For lack of warmth to smile on mouths of woe,
White as in chalk outlining little O,
Dumb, from a falling chin ;
Young, old, alike half-bent to make the hoop.

VIII

Their tongues of birds they wagged, weak-voiced as
        when
Dark underwaters the recesses choke ;
With cluck and upper quiver of a hen
In grasp, past pecking : cry before the croak.
Relentlessly their gold-haired Heaven, their fount
Bountiful of old days, heard them recount
This and that cruel stroke :
Nor eye nor ear had she for piteous men.

IX

A figure of black rock by sunbeams crowned
Through stormclouds, where the volumed shades
        enfold
An earth in awe before the claps resound
And woods and dwellings are as billows rolled.

The barren Nourisher unmelted shed
Death from the looks that wandered with the
    dead
Out of the realms of gold,
In famine for her lost, her lost unfound.

x

Iambe from her Mistress tripped ; she raised
The cattle-call above the moan of prayer ;
And slowly out of fields their fancy grazed,
Among the droves, defiled a horse and mare :
The wrecks of horse and mare : such ribs as view
Seas that have struck brave ships ashore, while
    through
Shoots the swift foamspit : bare
They nodded, and Demeter on them gazed.

xi

Howbeit the season of the dancing blood
Forgot was horse of mare, yea, mare of horse :
Reversed, each head at either's flank, they stood.
Whereat the Goddess, in a dim remorse,

Laid hand on them, and smacked; and her touch
    pricked.
Neighing within, at either's flank they licked;
Played on a moment's force
At courtship, withering to the crazy nod.

XII

The nod was that we gather for consent;
And mournfully amid the group a dame,
Interpreting the thing in nature meant,
Her hands held out like bearers of the flame,
And nodded for the negative sideways.
Keen at her Mistress glanced Iambe : rays
From the Great Mother came :
Her lips were opened wide; the curse was rent.

XIII

She laughed: since our first harvesting heard
    none
Like thunder of the song of heart : her face,
The dreadful darkness, shook to mounted sun,
And peal on peal across the hills held chase.

G

She laughed herself to water ; laughed to fire ;
Laughed the torrential laugh of dam and sire
Full of the marrowy race.
Her laughter, Gods ! was flesh on skeleton.

XIV

The valley people huddled, broke, afraid,
Assured, and taking lightning in the veins,
They puffed, they leaped, linked hands, together
    swayed,
Unwitting happiness till golden rains
Of tears in laughter, laughter weeping, smote
Knowledge of milky mercy from that throat
Pouring to heal their pains :
And one bold youth set mouth at a shy maid.

XV

Iambe clapped to see the kindly lusts
Inspire the valley people, still on seas,
Like poplar-tops relieved from stress of gusts,
With rapture in their wonderment ; but these,
Low homage being rendered, ran to plough,
Fed by the laugh, as by the mother cow
Calves at the teats they tease :
Soon drove they through the yielding furrow-crusts.

XVI

Uprose the blade in green, the leaf in red,
The tree of water and the tree of wood :
And soon among the branches overhead
Gave beauty juicy issue sweet for food.
O Laughter ! beauty plumped and love had birth.
Laughter ! O thou reviver of sick Earth !
Good for the spirit, good
For body, thou ! to both art wine and bread !

THE DAY OF THE DAUGHTER
OF HADES

I

He who has looked upon Earth
Deeper than flower and fruit,
Losing some hue of his mirth,
As the tree striking rock at the root,
Unto him shall the marvellous tale
Of Callistes more humanly come
With the touch on his breast than a hail
From the markets that hum.

II

Now the youth footed swift to the dawn.
'Twas the season when wintertide,
In the higher rock-hollows updrawn,
Leaves meadows to bud, and he spied,

100

By light throwing shallow shade,
Between the beam and the gloom,
Sicilian Enna, whose Maid
Such aspect wears in her bloom
Underneath since the Charioteer
Of Darkness whirled her away,
On a reaped afternoon of the year,
Nigh the poppy-droop of Day.
O and naked of her, all dust,
The majestic Mother and Nurse,
Ringing cries to the God, the Just,
Curled the land with the blight of her curse :
Recollected of this glad isle
Still quaking.   But now more fair,
And momently fraying the while
The veil of the shadows there,
Soft Enna that prostrate grief
Sang through, and revealed round the vines,
Bronze-orange, the crisp young leaf,
The wheat-blades tripping in lines,
A hue unillumined by sun
Of the flowers flooding grass as from founts :
All the penetrable dun
    Of the morn ere she mounts.

III

Nor had saffron and sapphire and red
Waved aloft to their sisters below,
When gaped by the rock-channel head
Of the lake, black, a cave at one blow,
Reverberant over the plain:
A sound oft fearfully swung
For the coming of wrathful rain:
And forth, like the dragon-tongue
Of a fire beaten flat by the gale,
But more as the smoke to behold,
A chariot burst. Then a wail
Quivered high of the love that would fold
Bliss immeasurable, bigger than heart,
Though a God's: and the wheels were
  stayed,
And the team of the chariot swart
Reared in marble, the six, dismayed,
Like hoofs that by night plashing sea
Curve and ramp from the vast swam-wave:
For, lo, the Great Mother, She!
And Callistes gazed, he gave
His eyeballs up to the sight:

The embrace of the Twain, of whom
To men are their day, their night,
Mellow fruits and the shearing tomb ·
Our Lady of the Sheaves
And the Lily of Hades, the Sweet
Of Enna : he saw through leaves
The Mother and Daughter meet.
They stood by the chariot-wheel,
Embraced, very tall, most like
Fellow poplars, wind-taken, that reel
Down their shivering columns and strike
Head to head, crossing throats : and apart,
For the feast of the look, they drew,
Which Darkness no longer could thwart ;
And they broke together anew,
Exulting to tears, flower and bud.
But the mate of the Rayless was grave :
·She smiled like Sleep on its flood,
That washes of all we crave :
Like the trance of eyes awake
And the spirit enshrouded, she cast
The wan underworld on the lake.
     They were so, and they passed.

IV

He tells it, who knew the law
Upon mortals: he stood alive
Declaring that this he saw:
    He could see, and survive.

V

Now the youth was not ware of the beams
With the grasses intertwined,
For each thing seen, as in dreams,
Came stepping to rear through his mind,
Till it struck his remembered prayer
To be witness of this which had flown
Like a smoke melted thinner than air,
That the vacancy doth disown.
And viewing a maiden, he thought
It might now be morn, and afar
Within him the memory wrought
Of a something that slipped from the car
When those, the august, moved by:
Perchance a scarf, and perchance
This maiden.　She did not fly,
Nor started at his advance:

She looked, as when infinite thirst
Pants pausing to bless the springs,
Refreshed, unsated.   Then first
He trembled with awe of the things
He had seen; and he did transfer,
Divining and doubting in turn,
His reverence unto her;
Nor asked what he crouched to learn:
The whence of her, whither, and why
Her presence there, and her name,
Her parentage: under which sky
Her birth, and how hither she came,
So young, a virgin, alone,
Unfriended, having no fear,
As Oreads have; no moan,
Like the lost upon earth; no tear;
Not a sign of the torch in the blood,
Though her stature had reached the height
When mantles a tender rud
In maids that of youths have sight,
If maids of our seed they be:
For he said: A glad vision art thou!
And she answered him: Thou to me
    As men utter a vow.

VI

Then said she, quick as the cries
Of the rainy cranes : Light ! light !
And Helios rose in her eyes,
That were full as the dew-balls bright,
Relucent to him as dews
Unshaded.   Breathing, she sent
Her voice to the God of the Muse,
And along the vale it went,
Strange to hear : not thin, not shrill .
Sweet, but no young maid's throat :
The echo beyond the hill
Ran falling on half the note :
And under the shaken ground
Where the Hundred-headed groans
By the roots of great Ætna bound,
As of him were hollow tones
Of wondering roared : a tale
Repeated to sunless halls.
But now off the face of the vale
Shadows fled in a breath, and the walls
Of the lake's rock-head were gold,
And the breast of the lake, that swell

Of the crestless long wave rolled
To shore-bubble, pebble and shell.
A morning of radiant lids
O'er the dance of the earth opened wide :
The bees chose their flowers, the snub kids
Upon hindlegs went sportive, or plied,
Nosing, hard at the dugs to be filled :
There was milk, honey, music to make :
Up their branches the little birds billed :
Chirrup, drone, bleat and buzz ringed the lake.
O shining in sunlight, chief
After water and water's caress,
Was the young bronze-orange leaf,
That clung to the tree as a tress,
Shooting lucid tendrils to wed
With the vine-hook tree or pole,
Like Arachne launched out on her thread.
Then the maiden her dusky stole
In the span of the black-starred zone,
Gathered up for her footing fleet.
As one that had toil of her own
She followed the lines of wheat
Tripping   straight   through   the   fields,   green
     blades,

To the groves of olive grey,
Downy-grey, golden-tinged : and to glades
Where the pear-blossom thickens the spray
In a night, like the snow-packed storm :
Pear, apple, almond, plum :
Not wintry now : pushing, warm !
And she touched them with finger and thumb,
As the vine-hook closes : she smiled,
Recounting again and again,
Corn, wine, fruit, oil ! like a child,
With the meaning known to men.
For hours in the track of the plough
And the pruning-knife she stepped,
And of how the seed works, and of how
Yields the soil, she seemed adept.
Then she murmured that name of the dearth,
The Beneficent, Hers, who bade
Our husbandmen sow for the birth
Of the grain making earth full glad.
She murmured that Other's : the dirge
Of life-light : for whose dark lap
Our locks are clipped on the verge
Of the realm where runs no sap.
She said : We have looked on both !

And her eyes had a wavering beam
Of various lights, like the froth
Of the storm-swollen ravine stream
In flame of the bolt.   What links
Were these which had made him her friend?
He eyed her, as one who drinks,
    And would drink to the end.

VII

Now the meadows with crocus besprent,
And the asphodel woodsides she left,
And the lake-slopes, the ravishing scent
Of narcissus, dark-sweet, for the cleft
That tutors the torrent-brook,
Delaying its forceful spleen
With many a wind and crook
Through rock to the broad ravine.
By the hyacinth-bells in the brakes,
And the shade-loved white windflower, half hid,
And the sun-loving lizards and snakes
On the cleft's barren ledges, that slid
Out of sight, smooth as waterdrops, all,
At a snap of twig or bark
In the track of the foreign foot-fall,

She climbed to the pineforest dark,
Overbrowing an emerald chine
Of the grass-billows.   Thence, as a wreath,
Running poplar and cypress to pine,
The lake-banks are seen, and beneath,
Vineyard, village, groves, rivers, towers, farms,
The citadel watching the bay,
The bay with the town in its arms,
The town shining white as the spray
Of the sapphire sea-wave on the rock,
Where the rock stars the girdle of sea,
White-ringed, as the midday flock,
Clipped by heat, rings the round of the tree.
That hour of the piercing shaft
Transfixes bough-shadows, confused
In veins of fire, and she laughed,
With her quiet mouth amused,
To see the whole flock, adroop,
Asleep, hug the tree-stem as one,
Imperceptibly filling the loop
Of its shade at a slant of sun.
The pipes under pent of the crag,
Where the goatherds in piping recline,
Have whimsical stops, burst and flag

Uncorrected as outstretched swine :
For the fingers are slack and unsure,
And the wind issues querulous :—thorns
And snakes !—but she listened demure,
Comparing day's music with morn's.
Of the gentle spirit that slips
From the bark of the tree she discoursed,
And of her of the wells, whose lips
Are coolness enchanting, rock-sourced.
And much of the sacred loon,
The frolic, the Goatfoot God,
For stories of indolent noon
In the pineforest's odorous nod,
She questioned, not knowing : he can
Be waspish, irascible, rude,
He is oftener friendly to man,
And ever to beasts and their brood.
For the which did she love him well,
She said, and his pipes of the reed,
His twitched lips puffing to tell
In music his tears and his need,
Against the sharp catch of his hurt.
Not as shepherds of Pan did she speak,
Nor spake as the schools, to divert,

But fondly, perceiving him weak
Before Gods, and to shepherds a fear,
A holiness, horn and heel.
All this she had learnt in her ear
From Callistes, and taught him to feel.
Yea, the solemn divinity flushed
Through the shaggy brown skin of the beast,
And the steeps where the cataract rushed,
And the wilds where the forest is priest,
Were his temple to clothe him in awe,
While she spake : 'twas a wonder : she read
The haunts of the beak and the claw
As plain as the land of bread,
But Cities and martial States,
Whither soon the youth veered his theme,
Were impervious barrier-gates
To her : and that ship, a trireme,
Nearing harbour, scarce wakened her glance,
Though he dwelt on the message it bore
Of sceptre and sword and lance
To the bee-swarms black on the shore,
Which were audible almost,
So black they were.   It befel
That he called up the warrior host

Of the Song pouring hydromel
In thunder, the wide-winged Song.
And he named with his boyish pride
The heroes, the noble throng
Past Acheron now, foul tide!
With his joy of the godlike band
And the verse divine, he named
The chiefs pressing hot on the strand,
Seen of Gods, of Gods aided, and maimed.
The fleetfoot and ireful; the King;
Him, the prompter in stratagem,
Many-shifted and masterful: Sing,
O Muse! But she cried: Not of them!
She breathed as if breath had failed,
And her eyes, while she bade him desist,
Held the lost-to-light ghosts grey-mailed,
As you see the grey river-mist
Hold shapes on the yonder bank.
A moment her body waned,
The light of her sprang and sank:
Then she looked at the sun, she regained
Clear feature, and she breathed deep.
She wore the wan smile he had seen,
As the flow of the river of Sleep,

On the mouth of the Shadow-Queen
In sunlight she craved to bask,
Saying: Life!   And who was she? who?
Of what issue?   He dared not ask,
     For that partly he knew.

VIII

A noise of the hollow ground
Turned the eye to the ear in debate:
Not the soft overflowing of sound
Of the pines, ranked, lofty, straight,
Barely swayed to some whispers remote,
Some swarming whispers above:
Not the pines with the faint airs afloat,
Hush-hushing the nested dove:
It was not the pines, or the rout
Oft heard from mid-forest in chase,
But the long muffled roar of a shout
Subterranean.   Sharp grew her face.
She rose, yet not moved by affright;
'Twas rather good haste to use
Her holiday of delight
In the beams of the God of the Muse.

And the steeps of the forest she crossed,
On its dry red sheddings and cones
Up the paths by roots green-mossed,
Spotted amber, and old mossed stones.
Then out where the brook-torrent starts
To her leap, and from bend to curve
A hurrying elbow darts
For the instant-glancing swerve,
Decisive, with violent will
In the action formed, like hers,
The maiden's, ascending; and still
Ascending, the bud of the furze,
The broom, and all blue-berried shoots
Of stubborn and prickly kind,
The juniper flat on its roots,
The dwarf rhododaphne, behind
She left, and the mountain sheep
Far behind, goat, herbage and flower.
The island was hers, and the deep,
All heaven, a golden hour.
Then with wonderful voice, that rang
Through air as the swan's nigh death,
Of the glory of Light she sang,
She sang of the rapture of Breath.

Nor ever, says he who heard,
Heard Earth in her boundaries broad,
From bosom of singer or bird
A sweetness thus rich of the God
Whose harmonies always are sane.
She sang of furrow and seed,
The burial, birth of the grain,
The growth, and the showers that feed,
And the green blades waxing mature
For the husbandman's armful brown.
O, the song in its burden ran pure,
And burden to song was a crown.
Callistes, a singer, skilled
In the gift he could measure and praise,
By a rival's art was thrilled,
Though she sang but a Song of Days,
Where the husbandman's toil and strife
Little varies to strife and toil :
But the milky kernel of life,
With her numbered : corn, wine, fruit, oil
The song did give him to eat :
Gave the first rapt vision of Good,
And the fresh young sense of Sweet
The grace of the battle for food,

With the issue Earth cannot refuse
When men to their labour are sworn.
'Twas a song of the God of the Muse
    To the forehead of Morn.

IX

Him loved she.   Lo, now was he veiled :
Over sea stood a swelled cloud-rack :
The fishing-boat havenward sailed,
Bent abeam, with a whitened track,
Surprised, fast hauling the net,
As it flew : sea dashed, earth shook.
She said : Is it night?   O not yet !
With a travail of thoughts in her look.
The mountain heaved up to its peak :
Sea darkened : earth gathered her fowl ;
Of bird or of branch rose the shriek.
Night? but never so fell a scowl
Wore night, nor the sky since then
When ocean ran swallowing shore,
And the Gods looked down for men.
Broke tempest with that stern roar

Never yet, save when black on the whirl
Rode wrath of a sovereign Power.
Then the youth and the shuddering girl,
Dim as shades in the angry shower,
Joined hands and descended a maze
Of the paths that were racing alive
Round boulder and bush, cleaving ways,
Incessant, with sound of a hive.
The height was a fountain-urn
Pouring streams, and the whole solid height
Leaped, chasing at every turn
The pair in one spirit of flight
To the folding pineforest.   Yet here,
Like the pause to things hunted, in doubt,
The stillness bred spectral fear
Of the awfulness ranging without,
And imminent.   Downward they fled,
From under the haunted roof,
To the valley aquake with the tread
Of an iron-resounding hoof,
As of legions of thunderful horse
Broken loose and in line tramping hard.
For the rage of a hungry force
Roamed blind of its mark over sward :

They saw it rush dense in the cloak
Of its travelling swathe of steam;
All the vale through a thin thread-smoke
Was thrown back to distance extreme:
And dull the full breast of it blinked,
Like a buckler of steel breathed o'er,
Diminished, in strangeness distinct,
Glowing cold, unearthly, hoar:
An Enna of fields beyond sun,
Out of light, in a lurid web;
And the traversing fury spun
Up and down with a wave's flow and ebb;
As the wave breaks to grasp and to spurn,
Retire, and in ravenous greed,
Inveterate, swell its return.
Up and down, as if wringing from speed
Sights that made the unsighted appear,
Delude and dissolve, on it scoured.
Lo, a sea upon land held career
Through the plain of the vale half-devoured.
Callistes of home and escape
Muttered swiftly, unwitting of speech.
She gazed at the Void of shape,
She put her white hand to his reach,

Saying : Now have we looked on the Three.
And divided·from day, from night,
From air that is breath, stood she,
    Like the vale, out of light.

x

Then again in disorderly words
He muttered of home, and was mute, .
With the heart of the cowering birds
Ere they burst off the fowler's foot.
He gave her some redness that streamed
Through her limbs in a flitting glow.
The sigh of our life she seemed,
The bliss of it clothing in woe.
Frailer than flower when the round
Of the sickle encircles it : strong
To tell of the things profound,
Our inmost uttering song,
Unspoken.   So stood she awhile
In the gloom of the terror afield,
And the silence about her smile
Said more than of tongue is revealed.
I have breathed : I have gazed : I have been :
It said : and not joylessly shone

The remembrance of light through the screen
Of a face that seemed shadow and stone.
She led the youth trembling, appalled,
To the lake-banks he saw sink and rise
Like a panic-struck breast.   Then she called,
And the hurricane blackness had eyes.
It launched like the Thunderer's bolt.
Pale she drooped, and the youth by her side
Would have clasped her and dared a revolt
Sacrilegious as ever defied
High Olympus, but vainly for strength
His compassionate heart shook a frame
Stricken rigid to ice all its length.
On amain the black traveller came.
Lo, a chariot, cleaving the storm,
Clove the fountaining lake with a plough,
And the lord of the steeds was in form
He, the God of implacable brow,
Darkness : he : he in person : he raged
Through the wave like a boar of the wilds
From the hunters and hounds disengaged,
And a name shouted hoarsely : his child's.
Horror melted in anguish to hear.
Lo, the wave hissed apart for the path

Of the terrible Charioteer,
With the foam and torn features of wrath,
Hurled aloft on each arm in a sheet ;
And the steeds clove it, rushing at land
Like the teeth of the famished at meat.
 Then he swept out his hand.

XI

This, no more, doth Callistes recall :
He saw, ere he dropped in swoon,
On the maiden the chariot fall,
As a thundercloud swings on the moon.
Forth, free of the deluge, one cry
From the vanishing gallop rose clear :
And : Skiágeneia ! the sky
Rang ; Skiágeneia ! the sphere.
And she left him therewith, to rejoice,
Repine, yearn, and know not his aim,
The life of their day in her voice,
 Left her life in her name.

XII

Now the valley in ruin of fields
And fair meadowland, showing at eve

Like the spear-pitted warrior's shields
After battle, bade men believe
That no other than wrathfullest God
Had been loose on her beautiful breast,
Where the flowery grass was clod,
Wheat and vine as a trailing nest.
The valley, discreet in grief,
Disclosed but the open truth,
And Enna had hope of the sheaf:
There was none for the desolate youth
Devoted to mourn and to crave.
Of the secret he had divined
Of his friend of a day would he rave ·
How for light of our earth she pined:
For the olive, the vine and the wheat,
Burning through with inherited fire:
And when Mother went Mother to meet,
She was prompted by simple desire
In the day-destined car to have place
At the skirts of the Goddess, unseen,
And be drawn to the dear earth's face.
She was fire for the blue and the green
Of our earth, dark fire; athirst
As a seed of her bosom for dawn,

White air that had robed and nursed
Her mother.   Now was she gone
With the Silent, the God without tear,
Like a bud peeping out of its sheath
To be sundered and stamped with the sere.
And Callistes to her beneath,
As she to our beams, extinct,
Strained arms: he was shade of her shade.
In division so were they linked.
But the song which had betrayed
Her flight to the cavernous ear
For its own keenly wakeful: that song
Of the sowing and reaping, and cheer
Of the husbandman's heart made strong
Through droughts and deluging rains
With his faith in the Great Mother's love:
O the joy of the breath she sustains,
And the lyre of the light above,
And the first rapt vision of Good,
And the fresh young sense of Sweet:
That song the youth ever pursued
In the track of her footing fleet.
For men to be profited much
By her day upon earth did he sing:

Of her voice, and her steps, and her touch
On the blossoms of tender Spring,
Immortal: and how in her soul
She is with them, and tearless abides,
Folding grain of a love for one goal
In patience, past flowing of tides.
And if unto him she was tears,
He wept not: he wasted within:
Seeming sane in the song, to his peers,
Only crazed where the cravings begin.
Our Lady of Gifts prized he less
Than her issue in darkness: the dim
Lost Skiágeneia's caress
Of our earth made it richest for him.
And for that was a curse on him raised,
And he withered rathe, dry to his prime,
Though the bounteous Giver be praised
Through the island with rites of old time
Exceedingly fervent, and reaped
Veneration for teachings devout,
Pious hymns when the corn-sheaves are heaped
And the wine-presses ruddily spout,
And the olive and apple are juice
At a touch light as hers lost below.

Whatsoever to men is of use
Sprang his worship of them who bestow,
In a measure of songs unexcelled :
But that soul loving earth and the sun
From her home of the shadows he held
For his beacon where beam there is none :
And to join her, or have her brought back,
In his frenzy the singer would call,
Till he followed where never was track,
    On the path trod of all.

THE YOUNG PRINCESS

A BALLAD OF OLD LAWS OF LOVE

I

I

WHEN the South sang like a nightingale
    Above a bower in May,
The training of Love's vine of flame
Was writ in laws, for lord and dame
    To say their yea and nay.

II

When the South sang like a nightingale
    Across the flowering night,
And lord and dame held gentle sport,
There came a young princess to Court,
    A frost of beauty white.

III

The South sang like a nightingale
　　To thaw her glittering dream:
No vine of Love her bosom gave,
She drank no wine of Love, but grave
　　She held them to Love's theme.

IV

The South grew all a nightingale
　　Beneath a moon unmoved:
Like the banner of war she led them on;
She left them to lie, like the light that has gone
　　From wine-cups overproved.

V

When the South was a fervid nightingale,
　　And she a chilling moon,
'Twas pity to see on the garden swards,
Against Love's laws, those rival lords
　　As willow-wands lie strewn.

VI

The South had throat of a nightingale
　　For her, the young princess:

She gave no vine of Love to rear,
Love's wine drank not, yet bent her ear
    To themes of Love no less.

II

I

THE lords of the Court they sighed heart-sick,
    Heart-free Lord Dusiote laughed:
I prize her no more than a fling o' the dice,
But, or shame to my manhood, a lady of ice,
    We master her by craft!

II

Heart-sick the lords of joyance yawned,
    Lord Dusiote laughed heart-free:
I count her as much as a crack o' my thumb,
But, or shame of my manhood, to me she shall come
    Like the bird to roost in the tree!

III

At dead of night when the palace-guard
    Had passed the measured rounds,

I

The young princess awoke to feel
A shudder of blood at the crackle of steel
   Within the garden-bounds.

IV

It ceased, and she thought of whom was need,
   The friar or the leech ;
When lo, stood her tirewoman breathless by :
Lord Dusiote, madam, to death is nigh,
   Of you he would have speech.

V

He prays you of your gentleness,
   To light him to his dark end.
The princess rose, and forth she went,
For charity was her intent,
   Devoutly to befriend.

VI

Lord Dusiote hung on his good squire's arm,
   The priest beside him knelt :
A weeping handkerchief was pressed
To stay the red flood at his breast,
   And bid cold ladies melt.

VII

O lady, though you are ice to men,
    All pure to heaven as light
Within the dew within the flower,
Of you 'tis whispered that love has power
    When secret is the night.

VIII

I have silenced the slanderers, peace to their souls !
    Save one was too cunning for me.
I die, whose love is late avowed,
He lives, who boasts the lily has bowed
    To the oath of a bended knee.

IX

Lord Dusiote drew breath with pain,
    And she with pain drew breath :
On him she looked, on his like above ;
She flew in the folds of a marvel of love
    Revealed to pass to death.

X

You are dying, O great-hearted lord,
    You are dying for me, she cried ;

O take my hand, O take my kiss,
And take of your right for love like this,
    The vow that plights me bride.

XI

She bade the priest recite his words
    While hand in hand were they,
Lord Dusiote's soul to waft to bliss ;
He had her hand, her vow, her kiss,
    And his body was borne away.

III

I

LORD DUSIOTE sprang from priest and squire ;
    He gazed at her lighted room :
The laughter in his heart grew slack ;
He knew not the force that pushed him back
    From her and the morn in bloom.

II

Like a drowned man's length on the strong
    flood-tide,
    Like the shade of a bird in the sun,

He fled from his lady whom he might claim
As ghost, and who made the daybeams flame
    To scare what he had done.

III

There was grief at Court for one so gay.
    Though he was a lord less keen
For training the vine than at vintage-press;
But in her soul the young princess
    Believed that love had been.

IV

Lord Dusiote fled the Court and land,
    He crossed the woeful seas,
Till his traitorous doing seemed clearer to burn,
And the lady beloved drew his heart for return,
    Like the banner of war in the breeze.

V

He neared the palace, he spied the Court,
    And music he heard, and they told
Of foreign lords arrived to bring
The nuptial gifts of a bridegroom king
    To the princess grave and cold.

VI

The masque and the dance were cloud on wave,
  And down the masque and the dance
Lord Dusiote stepped from dame to dame,
And to the young princess he came,
  With a bow and a burning glance.

VII

Do you take a new husband to-morrow, lady?
  She shrank as at prick of steel.
Must the first yield place to the second, he sighed.
Her eyes were like the grave that is wide
  For the corpse from head to heel.

VIII

My lady, my love, that little hand
  Has mine ringed fast in plight:
I bear for your lips a lawful thirst,
And as justly the second should follow the first,
  I come to your door this night.

IX

If a ghost should come a ghost will go:
  No more the lady said,

Save that ever when he in wrath began
To swear by the faith of a living man,
    She answered him, You are dead.

IV

I

THE soft night-wind went laden to death
    With smell of the orange in flower;
The light leaves prattled to neighbour ears;
The bird of the passion sang over his tears
    The night named hour by hour.

II

Sang loud, sang low the rapturous bird
    Till the yellow hour was nigh,
Behind the folds of a darker cloud:
He chuckled, he sobbed, alow, aloud;
    The voice between earth and sky.

III

O will you, will you, women are weak;
    The proudest are yielding mates

For a forward foot and a tongue of fire :
So thought Lord Dusiote's trusty squire,
  At watch by the palace-gates.

IV

The song of the bird was wine in his blood,
  And woman the odorous bloom :
His master's great adventure stirred
Within him to mingle the bloom and bird,
  And morn ere its coming illume.

V

Beside him strangely a piece of the dark
  Had moved, and the undertones
Of a priest in prayer, like a cavernous wave,
He heard, as were there a soul to save
  For urgency now in the groans.

VI

No priest was hired for the play this night :
  And the squire tossed head like a deer
At sniff of the tainted wind ; he gazed
Where cresset-lamps in a door were raised,
  Belike on a passing bier.

VII

All cloaked and masked, with naked blades,
    That flashed of a judgement done,
The lords of the Court, from the palace-door,
Came issuing silently, bearers four,
    And flat on their shoulders one.

VIII

They marched the body to squire and priest,
    They lowered it sad to earth:
The priest they gave the burial dole,
Bade wrestle hourly for his soul,
    Who was a lord of worth.

IX

One said, farewell to a gallant knight!
    And one, but a restless ghost!
'Tis a year and a day since in this place
He died, sped high by a lady of grace
    To join the blissful host.

X

Not vainly on us she charged her cause
    The lady whom we revere

For faith in the mask of a love untrue
To the Love we honour, the Love her due,
　　The Love we have vowed to rear.

XI

A trap for the sweet tooth, lures for the light,
　　For the fortress defiant a mine :
Right well !   But not in the South, princess,
Shall the lady snared of her nobleness
　　Ever shamed or a captive pine.

XII

When the South had voice of a nightingale
　　Above a Maying bower,
On the heights of Love walked radiant peers;
The bird of the passion sang over his tears
　　To the breeze and the orange-flower.

THE SONG OF THEODOLINDA

I

QUEEN THEODOLIND has built
In the earth a furnace-bed :
There the Traitor Nail that spilt
Blood of the anointed Head,
Red of heat, resolves in shame.
White of heat, awakes to flame.

       Beat, beat ! white of heat,
       Red of heat, beat, beat !

II

Mark the skeleton of fire
Lightening from its thunder-roof :
So comes this that saw expire
Him we love, for our behoof !
Red of heat, O white of heat,
This from off the Cross we greet.

III

Brown-cowled hammermen around
Nerve their naked arms to strike
Death with Resurrection crowned,
Each upon that cruel spike.
Red of heat the furnace leaps,
White of heat transfigured sleeps.

IV

Hard against the furnace core
Holds the Queen her streaming eyes :
Lo ! that thing of piteous gore
In the lap of radiance lies,
Red of heat, as when He takes,
White of heat, whom earth forsakes.

V

Forth with it, and crushing ring
Iron hymns, for men to hear
Echoes of the deeds that sting
Earth into its graves, and fear !
Red of heat, He maketh thus,
White of heat, a crown of us.

VI

This that killed Thee, kissed Thee, Lord!
Touched Thee, and we touch it: dear,
Dark it is; adored, abhorred:
Vilest, yet most sainted here.
Red of heat, O white of heat,
In it hell and heaven meet.

VII

I behold our morning day
When they chased Him out with rods
Up to where this traitor lay
Thirsting; and the blood was God's!
Red of heat, it shall be pressed,
White of heat, once on my breast!

VIII

Quick! the reptile in me shrieks,
Not the soul. Again; the Cross
Burn there. Oh! this pain it wreaks
Rapture is: pain is not loss.
Red of heat, the tooth of Death,
White of heat, has caught my breath.

IX

Brand me, bite me, bitter thing!
Thus He felt, and thus I am
One with Him in suffering,
One with Him in bliss, the Lamb.
Red of heat, O white of heat,
Thus is bitterness made sweet.

X

Now am I, who bear that stamp
Scorched in me, the living sign
Sole on earth—the lighted lamp
Of the dreadful Day divine.
White of heat, beat on it fast!
Red of heat, its shape has passed.

XI

Out in angry sparks they fly,
They that sentenced Him to bleed:
Pontius and his troop: they die,
Damned for ever for the deed!
White of heat in vain they soar:
Red of heat they strew the floor.

XII

Fury on it! have its debt!
Thunder on the Hill accurst,
Golgotha, be ye! and sweat
Blood, and thirst the Passion's thirst.
Red of heat and white of heat,
Champ it like fierce teeth that eat.

XIII

Strike it as the ages crush
Towers! for while a shape is seen
I am rivalled.   Quench its blush,
Devil!   But it crowns me Queen,
Red of heat, as none before,
White of heat, the circlet wore.

XIV

Lowly I will be, and quail,
Crawling, with a beggar's hand.
On my breast the branded Nail,
On my head the iron band.   ·
Red of heat, are none so base!
White of heat, none know such grace!

XV

In their heaven the sainted hosts,
Robed in violet unflecked,
Gaze on humankind as ghosts:
I draw down a ray direct.
Red of heat, across my brow,
White of heat, I touch Him now.

XVI

Robed in violet, robed in gold,
Robed in pearl, they make our dawn.
What am I to them?   Behold
What ye are to me, and fawn.
Red of heat, be humble, ye !
White of heat, O teach it me '

XVII

Martyrs ! hungry peaks in air,
Rent with lightnings, clad with snow,
Crowned with stars ! you strip me bare,
Pierce me, shame me, stretch me low,
Red of heat, but it may be,
White of heat, some envy me !

XVIII

O poor enviers! God's own gifts
Have a devil for the weak.
Yea, the very force that lifts
Finds the vessel's secret leak.
Red of heat, I rise o'er all:
White of heat, I faint, I fall.

XIX

Those old Martyrs sloughed their pride,
Taking humbleness like mirth.
I am to His Glory tied,
I that witness Him on earth!
Red of heat, my pride of dust,
White of heat, feeds fire in trust

XX

Kindle me to constant fire,
Lest the nail be but a nail!
Give me wings of great desire,
Lest I look within, and fail!
Red of heat, the furnace light,
White of heat, fix on my sight.

K

XXI

Never for the Chosen peace !
Know, by me tormented know,
Never shall the wrestling cease
Till with our outlasting Foe,
Red of heat to white of heat,
Roll we to the Godhead's feet !
   Beat, beat ! white of heat,
   Red of heat, beat, beat !

THE NUPTIALS OF ATTILA

FLAT as to an eagle's eye,
    Earth hung under Attila.
Sign for carnage gave he none.
In the peace of his disdain,
Sun and rain, and rain and sun,
Cherished men to wax again,
Crawl, and in their manner die.
On his people stood a frost.
Like the charger cut in stone,
Rearing stiff, the warrior host,
Which had life from him alone,
Craved the trumpet's eager note,
As the bridled earth the Spring.
Rusty was the trumpet's throat.
He let chief and prophet rave;
Venturous earth around him string

147

Threads of grass and slender rye,
Wave them, and untrampled wave.
O foi the time when God did cry,
    Eye and have, my Attila!

II

Scorn of conquest filled like sleep
Him that drank of havoc deep
When the Green Cat pawed the globe:
When the horsemen from his bow
Shot in sheaves and made the foe
Crimson fringes of a robe,
Trailed o'er towns and fields in woe;
When they streaked the rivers red,
When the saddle was the bed.
    Attila, my Attila!

III

He breathed peace and pulled a flower.
    Eye and have, my Attila!
This was the damsel Ildico,
Rich in bloom until that hour:

Shyer than the forest doe
Twinkling slim through branches green.
Yet the shyest shall be seen.
          Make the bed for Attila !

IV

Seen of Attila, desired,
She was led to him straightway :
Radiantly was she attired ;
Rifled lands were her array,
Jewels bled from weeping crowns,
Gold of woeful fields and towns.
She stood pallid in the light.
How she walked, how withered white,
From the blessing to the board,
She who would have proudly blushed,
Women whispered, asking why,
Hinting of a youth, and hushed.
Was it terror of her lord ?
Was she childish ? was she sly ?
Was it the bright mantle's dye
Drained her blood to hues of grief
Like the ash that shoots the spark ?

See the green tree all in leaf:
See the green tree stripped of bark !—
    Make the bed for Attila ;

V

Round the banquet-table's load
Scores of iron horsemen rode ;
Chosen warriors, keen and hard ;
Grain of threshing battle-dints ;
Attila's fierce body-guard,
Smelling war like fire in flints.
Grant them peace be fugitive !
Iron-capped and iron-heeled,
Each against his fellow's shield
Smote the spear-head, shouting, Live,
    Attila ! my Attila !
Eagle, eagle of our breed,
Eagle, beak the lamb, and feed !
Have her, and unleash us ! live,
    Attila ! my Attila !

VI

He was of the blood to shine
Bronze in joy, like skies that scorch.

Beaming with the goblet wine
In the wavering of the torch,
Looked he backward on his bride.
    Eye and have, my Attila!
Fair in her wide robe was she:
Where the robe and vest divide,
Fair she seemed surpassingly:
Soft, yet vivid as the stream
Danube rolls in the moonbeam
Through rock-barriers: but she smiled
Never, she sat cold as salt:
Open-mouthed as a young child
Wondering with a mind at fault.
    Make the bed for Attila!

VII

Under the thin hoop of gold
Whence in waves her hair outrolled,
'Twixt her brows the women saw
Shadows of a vulture's claw
Gript in flight: strange knots that sped
Closing and dissolving aye:
Such as wicked dreams betray
When pale dawn creeps o'er the bed.

They might show the common pang
Known to virgins, in whom dread
Hunts their bliss like famished hounds;
While the chiefs with roaring rounds
Tossed her to her lord, and sang
Praise of him whose hand was large,
Cheers for beauty brought to yield,
Chirrups of the trot afield,
Hurrahs of the battle-charge.

VIII

Those rock-faces hung with weed
Reddened: their great days of speed,
Slaughter, triumph, flood and flame,
Like a jealous frenzy wrought,
Scoffed at them and did them shame,
Quaffing idle, conquering nought.
O for the time when God decreed
    Earth the prey of Attila!
God called on thee in his wrath,
Trample it to mire!   'Twas done.
Swift as Danube clove our path
Down from East to Western sun.

Huns ! behold your pasture, gaze,
Take, our king said : heel to flank
(Whisper it, the war-horse neighs !)
Forth we drove, and blood we drank
Fresh as dawn-dew : earth was ours :
Men were flocks we lashed and spurned :
Fast as windy flame devours,
Flame along the wind, we burned.
Arrow, javelin, spear, and sword !
Here the snows and there the plains ;
On ! our signal : onward poured
Torrents of the tightened reins,
Foaming over vine and corn
Hot against the city-wall.
Whisper it, you sound a horn
To the grey beast in the stall !
Yea, he whinnies at a nod.
O for sound of the trumpet-notes !
O for the time when thunder-shod,
He that scarce can munch his oats,
Hung on the peaks, brooded aloof,
Champed the grain of the wrath of God,
Pressed a cloud on the cowering roof,
Snorted out of the blackness fire !

Scarlet broke the sky, and down,
Hammering West with print of his hoof,
He burst out of the bosom of ire
Sharp as eyelight under thy frown,
  Attila, my Attila!

IX

Ravaged cities rolling smoke
Thick on cornfields dry and black,
Wave his banners, bear his yoke.
Track the lightning, and you track
Attila. They moan: 'tis he!
Bleed: 'tis he! Beneath his foot
Leagues are deserts charred and mute;
Where he passed, there passed a sea.
  Attila, my Attila!

X

—Who breathed on the king cold breath?
Said a voice amid the host,
He is Death that weds a ghost,
Else a ghost that weds with Death?
Ildico's chill little hand
Shuddering he beheld: austere

Stared, as one who would command
Sight of what has filled his ear:
Plucked his thin beard, laughed disdain.
Feast, ye Huns!   His arm be raised,
Like the warrior, battle-dazed,
Joining to the fight amain.
     Make the bed for Attila!

XI

Silent Ildico stood up.
King and chief to pledge her well,
Shocked sword sword and cup on cup,
Clamouring like a brazen bell.
Silent stepped the queenly slave.
Fair, by heaven! she was to meet
On a midnight, near a grave,
Flapping wide the winding-sheet.

XII

Death and she walked through the crowd,
Out beyond the flush of light.
Ceremonious women bowed
Following her: 'twas middle night.

Then the warriors each on each
Spied, nor overloudly laughed ;
Like the victims of the leech,
Who have drunk of a strange draught.

XIII

Attila remained.   Even so
Frowned he when he struck the blow,
Brained his horse, that stumbled twice
On a bloody day in Gaul,
Bellowing, Perish omens !   All
Marvelled at the sacrifice,
But the battle, swinging dim,
Rang off that axe-blow for him.
      Attila, my Attila !

XIV

Brightening over Danube wheeled
Star by star ; and she, most fair,
Sweet as victory half-revealed,
Seized to make him glad and young ;
She, O sweet as the dark sign
Given him oft in battles gone,

When the voice within said, Dare!
And the trumpet-notes were sprung
Rapturous for the charge in line:
She lay waiting: fair as dawn
Wrapped in folds of night she lay;
Secret, lustrous; flaglike there,
Waiting him to stream and ray,
With one loosening blush outflung,
Colours of his hordes of horse
Ranked for combat; still he hung
Like the fever dreading air,
Cursed of heat; and as a corse
Gathers vultures, in his brain
Images of her eyes and kiss
Plucked at the limbs that could remain
Loitering nigh the doors of bliss.
  Make the bed for Attila!

XV

Passion on one hand, on one,
Destiny led forth the Hun.
Heard ye outcries of affright,
Voices that through many a fray,

In the press of flag and spear,
Warned the king of peril near?
Men were dumb, they gave him way,
Eager heads to left and right,
Like the bearded standard, thrust,
As in battle, for a nod
From their lord of battle-dust.
    Attila, my Attila!
Slow between the lines he trod.
Saw ye not the sun drop slow
On this nuptial day, ere eve
Pierced him on the couch aglow?
    Attila, my Attila!
Here and there his heart would cleave
Clotted memory for a space:
Some stout chief's familiar face,
Choicest of his fighting brood,
Touched him, as 'twere one to know
Ere he met his bride's embrace.
    Attila, my Attila!
Twisting fingers in a beard
Scant as winter underwood,
With a narrowed eye he peered;
Like the sunset's graver red

Up old pine-stems.   Grave he stood
Eyeing them on whom was shed
Burning light from him alone.
　　Attila, my Attila !
Red were they whose mouths recalled
Where the slaughter mounted high,
High on it, o'er earth appalled,
He ; heaven's finger in their sight
Raising him on waves of dead,
Up to heaven his trumpets blown.
O for the time when God's delight
　　Crowned the head of Attila !
Hungry river of the crag
Stretching hands for earth he came :
Force and Speed astride his name
Pointed back to spear and flag.
He came out of miracle cloud,
Lightning-swift and spectre-lean.
Now those days are in a shroud :
Have him to his ghostly queen.
　　Make the bed for Attila !

XVI

One, with winecups overstrung,
Cried him farewell in Rome's tongue.

Who? for the great king turned as though
Wrath to the shaft's head strained the
    bow.
Nay, not wrath the king possessed,
But a radiance of the breast.
In that sound he had the key
Of his cunning malady.
Lo, where gleamed the sapphire lake,
Leo, with his Rome at stake,
Drew blank air to hues and forms;
Whereof Two that shone distinct,
Linked as orbed stars are linked,
Clear among the myriad swarms,
In a constellation, dashed
Full on horse and rider's eyes
Sunless light, but light it was—
Light that blinded and abashed,
Froze his members, bade him pause,
Caught him mid-gallop, blazed him home.
    Attila, my Attila!
What are streams that cease to flow?
What was Attila, rolled thence,
Cheated by a juggler's show?
Like that lake of blue intense,

Under tempest lashed to foam,
Lurid radiance, as he passed,
Filled him, and around was glassed,
When deep-voiced he uttered, Rome!

XVII

Rome! the word was : and like meat
Flung to dogs the word was torn.
Soon Rome's magic priests shall bleat
Round their magic Pope forlorn!
Loud they swore the king had sworn
Vengeance on the Roman cheat,
Ere he passed, as, grave and still,
Danube through the shouting hill.
Sworn it by his naked life!
Eagle, snakes these women are:
Take them on the wing! but war,
Smoking war's the warrior's wife!
Then for plunder! then for brides
Won without a winking priest!—
Danube whirled his train of tides
Black toward the yellow East.

    Make the bed for Attila!

XVIII

Chirrups of the trot afield,
Hurrahs of the battle-charge,
How they answered, how they pealed,
When the morning rose and drew
Bow and javelin, lance and targe,
In the nuptial casement's view !
    Attila, my Attila !
Down the hillspurs, out of tents
Glimmering in mid-forest, through
Mists of the cool morning scents,
Forth from city-alley, court,
Arch, the bounding horsemen flew,
Joined along the plains of dew,
Raced and gave the rein to sport,
Closed and streamed like curtain-rents
Fluttered by a wind, and flowed
Into squadrons : trumpets blew,
Chargers neighed, and trappings glowed
Brave as the bright Orient's.
Look on the seas that run to greet
Sunrise : look on the leagues of wheat ·
Look on the lines and squares that fret
Leaping to level the lance blood-wet.

Tens of thousands, man and steed,
Tossing like field-flowers in Spring;
Ready to be hurled at need
Whither their great lord may sling.
Finger Romeward, Romeward, King!
    Attila, my Attila!
Still the woman holds him fast
As a night-flag round the mast.

XIX

Nigh upon the fiery noon,
Out of ranks a roaring burst.
'Ware white women like the moon!
They are poison: they have thirst
First for love, and next for rule.
Jealous of the army, she?
Ho, the little wanton fool!
We were his before she squealed
Blind for mother's milk, and heeled
Kicking on her mother's knee.
His in life and death are we:
She but one flower of a field.
We have given him bliss tenfold

In an hour to match her night:
    Attila, my Attila!
Still her arms the master hold,
As on wounds the scarf winds tight.

XX

Over Danube day no more,
Like the warrior's planted spear,
Stood to hail the King: in fear
Western day knocked at his door.
    Attila, my Attila!
Sudden in the army's eyes
Rolled a blast of lights and cries:
Flashing through them: Dead are ye!
Dead, ye Huns, and torn piecemeal!
See the ordered army reel
Stricken through the ribs: and see,
Wild for speed to cheat despair,
Horsemen, clutching knee to chin,
Crouch and dart they know not where.
    Attila, my Attila!
Faces covered, faces bare,
Light the palace-front like jets
Of a dreadful fire within.

Beating hands and driving hair
Start on roof and parapets.
Dust rolls up; the slaughter din.
—Death to them who call him dead!
Death to them who doubt the tale!
Choking in his dusty veil,
Sank the sun on his death-bed.
    Make the bed for Attila!

XXI

'Tis the room where thunder sleeps.
Frenzy, as a wave to shore
Surging, burst the silent door,
And drew back to awful deeps
Breath beaten out, foam-white.   Anew
Howled and pressed the ghastly crew,
Like storm-waters over rocks.
    Attila, my Attila!
One long shaft of sunset red
Laid a finger on the bed.
Horror, with the snaky locks,
Shocked the surge to stiffened heaps,
Hoary as the glacier's head

Faced to the moon.   Insane they look.
God it is in heaven who weeps
Fallen from his hand the Scourge he shook.
        Make the bed for Attila !

XXII

Square along the couch, and stark,
Like the sea-rejected thing
Sea-sucked white, behold their King.
        Attila, my Attila !
Beams that panted black and bright,
Scornful lightnings danced their sight :
Him they see an oak in bud,
Him an oaklog stripped of bark :
Him, their lord of day and night,
White, and lifting up his blood
Dumb for vengeance.   Name us that,
Huddled in the corner dark,
Humped and grinning like a cat,
Teeth for lips !—'tis she ! she stares,
Glittering through her bristled hairs.
Rend her !   Pierce her to the hilt !
She is Murder : have her out.

What ! this little fist, as big
As the southern summer fig !
She is Madness, none may doubt.
Death, who dares deny her guilt .
Death, who says his blood she spilt '
    Make the bed for Attila !

XXIII

Torch and lamp and sunset-red
Fell three-fingered on the bed.
In the torch the beard-hair scant
With the great breast seemed to pant :
In the yellow lamp the limbs
Wavered, as the lake-flower swims :
In the sunset red the dead
Dead avowed him, dry blood-red.

XXIV

Hatred of that abject slave,
Earth, was in each chieftain's heart.
Earth has got him, whom God gave,
Earth may sing, and earth shall smart
    Attila, my Attila !

XXV

Thus their prayer was raved and ceased.
Then had Vengeance of her feast
Scent in their quick pang to smite
Which they knew not, but huge pain
Urged them for some victim slain
Swift, and blotted from the sight.
Each at each, a crouching beast,
Glared, and quivered for the word.
Each at each, and all on that,
Humped and grinning like a cat,
Head-bound with its bridal-wreath.
Then the bitter chamber heard
Vengeance in a cauldron seethe.
Hurried counsel rage and craft
Yelped to hungry men, whose teeth
Hard the grey lip-ringlet gnawed,
Gleaming till their fury laughed.
With the steel-hilt in the clutch,
Eyes were shot on her that froze
In their blood-thirst overawed ;
Burned to rend, yet feared to touch.
She that was his nuptial rose,
She was of his heart's blood clad :

Oh ! the last of him she had !—
Could a little fist as big
As the southern summer fig,
Push a dagger's point to pierce
Ribs like those ?   Who else !   They glared
Each at each.   Suspicion fierce
Many a black remembrance bared.

     Attila, my Attila !
Death, who dares deny her guilt !
Death, who says his blood she spilt !
Traitor he, who stands between !
Swift to hell, who harms the Queen !
She, the wild contention's cause,
Combed her hair with quiet paws.
     Make the bed for Attila !

XXVI

Night was on the host in arms.
Night, as never night before,
Hearkened to an army's roar
Breaking up in snaky swarms :
Torch and steel and snorting steed,
Hunted by the cry of blood,

Cursed with blindness, mad for day.
Where the torches ran a flood,
Tales of him and of the deed
Showered like a torrent spray.
Fear of silence made them strive
Loud in warrior-hymns that grew
Hoarse for slaughter yet unwreaked.
Ghostly Night across the hive,
With a crimson finger drew
Letters on her breast and shrieked.
Night was on them like the mould
On the buried half alive.
Night, their bloody Queen, her fold
Wound on them and struck them through.
      Make the bed for Attila !

XXVII

Earth has got him whom God gave,
Earth may sing, and earth shall smart !
None of earth shall know his grave.
They that dig with Death depart.
      Attila, my Attila !

XXVIII

Thus their prayer was raved and passed :
Passed in peace their red sunset :
Hewn and earthed those men of sweat
Who had housed him in the vast,
Where no mortal might declare,
There lies he—his end was there !
    Attila, my Attila !

XXIX

Kingless was the army left :
Of its head the race bereft.
Every fury of the pit
Tortured and dismembered it.
Lo, upon a silent hour,
When the pitch of frost subsides,
Danube with a shout of power
Loosens his imprisoned tides :
Wide around the frighted plains
Shake to hear his riven chains,
Dreadfuller than heaven in wrath,
As he makes himself a path :
High leap the ice-cracks, towering pile
Floes to bergs, and giant peers

Wrestle on a drifted isle;
Island on ice-island rears;
Dissolution battles fast:
Big the senseless Titans loom,
Through a mist of common doom
Striving which shall die the last:
Till a gentle-breathing morn
Frees the stream from bank to bank.
So the Empire built of scorn
Agonized, dissolved and sank.
Of the Queen no more was told
Than of leaf on Danube rolled.
    Make the bed for Attila!

PENETRATION AND TRUST

I

Sleek as a lizard at round of a stone,
The look of her heart slipped out and in.
Sweet on her lord her soft eyes shone,
As innocents clear of a shade of sin.

II

He laid a finger under her chin,
His arm for her girdle at waist was thrown
Now, what will happen and who will win,
With me in the fight and my lady lone?

III

He clasped her, clasping a shape of stone;
Was fire on her eyes till they let him in.
Her breast to a God of the daybeams shone,
And never a corner for serpent sin.

IV

Tranced she stood, with a chattering chin;
Her shrunken form at his feet was thrown:
At home to the death my lord shall win,
When it is no tyrant who leaves me lone

LUCIFER IN STARLIGHT

On a starred night Prince Lucifer uprose.
Tired of his dark dominion swung the fiend
Above the rolling ball in cloud part screened,
Where sinners hugged their spectre of repose.
Poor prey to his hot fit of pride were those.
And now upon his western wing he leaned,
Now his huge bulk o'er Afric's sands careened,
Now the black planet shadowed Arctic snows.
Soaring through wider zones that pricked his scars
With memory of the old revolt from Awe,
He reached a middle height, and at the stars,
Which are the brain of heaven, he looked, and sank.
Around the ancient track marched, rank on rank,
The army of unalterable law.

THE STAR SIRIUS

Bright Sirius ! that when Orion pales
To dotlings under moonlight still art keen
With cheerful fervour of a warrior's mien
Who holds in his great heart the battle-scales :
Unquenched of flame though swift the flood
     assails,
Reducing many lustrous to the lean :
Be thou my star, and thou in me be seen
To show what source divine is, and prevails.
Long watches through, at one with godly night,
I mark thee planting joy in constant fire ;
And thy quick beams, whose jets of life inspire
Life to the spirit, passion for the light,
Dark Earth since first she lost her lord from sight
Has viewed and felt them sweep her as a lyre.

THE SPIRIT OF SHAKESPEARE

THY greatest knew thee, Mother Earth; unsoured
He knew thy sons.   He probed from hell to hell
Of human passions, but of love deflowered
His wisdom was not, for he knew thee well.
Thence came the honeyed corner at his lips,
The conquering smile wherein his spirit sails
Calm as the God who the white sea-wave whips,
Yet full of speech and intershifting tales,
Close mirrors of us : thence had he the laugh
We feel is thine : broad as ten thousand beeves
At pasture ! thence thy songs, that winnow chaff
From grain, bid sick Philosophy's last leaves
Whirl, if they have no response—they enforced
To fatten Earth when from her soul divorced.

Continued

How smiles he at a generation ranked
In gloomy noddings over life !   They pass.
Not he to feed upon a breast unthanked,
Or eye a beauteous face in a cracked glass.
But he can spy that little twist of brain
Which moved some weighty leader of the blind,
Unwitting 'twas the goad of personal pain,
To view in curst eclipse our Mother's mind,
And show us of some rigid harridan
The wretched bondmen till the end of time.
O lived the Master now to paint us Man,
That little twist of brain would ring a chime
Of whence it came and what it caused, to start
Thunders of laughter, clearing air and heart.

THE WORLD'S ADVANCE

JUDGE mildly the tasked world; and disincline
To brand it, for it bears a heavy pack.
You have perchance observed the inebriate's track
At night when he has quitted the inn-sign :
He plays diversions on the homeward line,
Still that way bent albeit his legs are slack :
A hedge may take him, but he turns not back,
Nor turns this burdened world, of curving spine.
'Spiral,' the memorable Lady terms
Our mind's ascent: our world's advance presents
That figure on a flat; the way of worms.
Cherish the promise of its good intents,
And warn it, not one instinct to efface
Ere Reason ripens for the vacant place.

EARTH'S SECRET

Nor solitarily in fields we find
Earth's secret open, though one page is there;
Her plainest, such as children spell, and share
With bird and beast; raised letters for the blind.
Not where the troubled passions toss the mind,
In turbid cities, can the key be bare.
It hangs for those who hither thither fare,
Close interthreading nature with our kind.
They, hearing History speak, of what men were,
And have become, are wise.   The gain is great
In vision and solidity; it lives.
Yet at a thought of life apart from her,
Solidity and vision lose their state,
For Earth, that gives the milk, the spirit gives.

SENSE AND SPIRIT

THE senses loving Earth or well or ill,
Ravel yet more the riddle of our lot.
The mind is in their trammels, and lights not
By trimming fear-bred tales ; nor does the will
To find in nature things which less may chill
An ardour that desires, unknowing what.
Till we conceive her living we go distraught,
At best but circle-windsails of a mill.
Seeing she lives, and of her joy of life
Creatively has given us blood and breath
For endless war and never wound unhealed,
The gloomy Wherefore of our battle-field
Solves in the Spirit, wrought of her through strife
To read her own and trust her down to death.

GRACE AND LOVE

Two flower-enfolding crystal vases she
I love fills daily, mindful but of one :
And close behind pale morn she, like the sun
Priming our world with light, pours, sweet to see,
Clear water in the cup, and into me
The image of herself: and that being done,
Choice of what blooms round her fair garden run
In climbers or in creepers or the tree,
She ranges with unerring fingers fine,
To harmony so vivid that through sight
I hear, I have her heavenliness to fold
Beyond the senses, where such love as mine,
Such grace as hers, should the strange Fates with-
    hold
Their starry more from her and me, unite.

WINTER HEAVENS

Sharp is the night, but stars with frost alive,
Leap off the rim of earth across the dome.
It is a night to make the heavens our home
More than the nest whereto apace we strive.
Lengths down our road each fir-tree seems a hive,
In swarms outrushing from the golden comb.
They waken waves of thoughts that burst to foam:
The living throb in me, the dead revive.
Yon mantle clothes us: there, past mortal breath,
Life glistens on the river of the death.
It folds us flesh and dust; and have we knelt,
Or never knelt, or eyed as kine the springs
Of radiance, the radiance enrings:
And this is the soul's haven to have felt.

MODERN LOVE

In our old shipwrecked days there was an hour,
When in the firelight steadily aglow,
Joined slackly, we beheld the red chasm grow
Among the clicking coals. Our library-bower
That eve was left to us; and hushed we sat
As lovers to whom Time is whispering.
From sudden-opened doors we heard them sing :
The nodding elders mixed good wine with chat.
Well knew we that Life's greatest treasure lay
With us, and of it was our talk.   'Ah, yes !
Love dies !' I said : I never thought it less.
She yearned to me that sentence to unsay.
Then when the fire domed blackening, I found
Her cheek was salt against my kiss, and swift
Up the sharp scale of sobs her breast did lift :—
Now am I haunted by that taste ! that sound !

184

43

Mark where the pressing wind shoots javelin-like,
Its skeleton shadow on the broad-backed wave !
Here is a fitting spot to dig Love's grave ;
Here where the ponderous breakers plunge and
   strike,
And dart their hissing tongues high up the sand ;
In hearing of the ocean, and in sight
Of those ribbed wind-streaks running into white.
If I the death of Love had deeply planned,
I never could have made it half so sure,
As by the unblest kisses which upbraid
The full-waked sense ; or failing that, degrade !
'Tis morning : but no morning can restore
What we have forfeited.   I see no sin :
The wrong is mixed.   In tragic life, God wot,
No villain need be !   Passions spin the plot :
We are betrayed by what is false within.

We saw the swallows gathering in the sky,
And in the osier-isle we heard their noise.
We had not to look back on Summer joys,
Or forward to a Summer of bright dye :
But in the largeness of the evening earth
Our spirits grew as we went side by side.
The hour became her husband and my bride.
Love that had robbed us so, thus blessed our
    dearth !
The pilgrims of the year waxed very loud
In multitudinous chatterings, as the flood
Full brown came from the West, and like pale blood
Expanded to the upper crimson cloud.
Love that had robbed us of immortal things,
This little moment mercifully gave,
Where I have seen across the twilight wave
The swan sail with her young beneath her wings.

50

Thus piteously Love closed what he begat:
The union of this ever-diverse pair!
These two were rapid falcons in a snare,
Condemned to do the flitting of the bat.
Lovers beneath the singing sky of May,
They wandered once; clear as the dew on flowers.
But they fed not on the advancing hours:
Their hearts held cravings for the buried day.
Then each applied to each that fatal knife,
Deep questioning, which probes to endless dole.
Ah, what a dusty answer gets the soul
When hot for certainties in this our life!—
In tragic hints here see what evermore
Moves dark as yonder midnight ocean's force,
Thundering like ramping hosts of warrior horse,
To throw that faint thin line upon the shore!

JUGGLING JERRY

I

P<small>ITCH</small> here the tent, while the old horse grazes .
By the old hedge-side we'll halt a stage.
It's nigh my last above the daisies :
My next leaf 'll be man's blank page.
Yes, my old girl! and it's no use crying :
Juggler, constable, king, must bow.
One that outjuggles all's been spying
Long to have me, and he has me now.

II

We've travelled times to this old common :
Often we've hung our pots in the gorse.
We've had a stirring life, old woman !
You, and I, and the old grey horse.
Races, and fairs, and royal occasions,
Found us coming to their call :
Now they'll miss us at our stations :
There's a Juggler outjuggles all !

III

Up goes the lark, as if all were jolly!
  Over the duck-pond the willow shakes.
Easy to think that grieving's folly,
  When the hand's firm as driven stakes!
Ay, when we're strong, and braced, and manful,
  Life's a sweet fiddle: but we're a batch
Born to become the Great Juggler's han'ful:
  Balls he shies up, and is safe to catch.

IV

Here's where the lads of the village cricket:
  I was a lad not wide from here:
Couldn't I whip off the bail from the wicket?
  Like an old world those days appear!
Donkey, sheep, geese, and thatched ale-house—
  I know them!
They are old friends of my halts, and seem,
  Somehow, as if kind thanks I owe them:
Juggling don't hinder the heart's esteem.

V

Juggling's no sin, for we must have victual:
  Nature allows us to bait for the fool.

Holding one's own makes us juggle no little;
  But, to increase it, hard juggling 's the rule.
You that are sneering at my profession,
  Haven't you juggled a vast amount?
There's the Prime Minister, in one Session,
  Juggles more games than my sins 'll count.

VI

I've murdered insects with mock thunder:
  Conscience, for that, in men don't quail.
I've made bread from the bump of wonder:
  That's my business, and there's my tale.
Fashion and rank all praised the professor:
  Ay! and I've had my smile from the Queen:
Bravo, Jerry! she meant: God bless her!
  Ain't this a sermon on that scene?

VII

I've studied men from my topsy-turvy
  Close, and, I reckon, rather true.
Some are fine fellows: some, right scurvy:
  Most, a dash between the two.

But it's a woman, old girl, that makes me
　Think more kindly of the race :
And it's a woman, old girl, that shakes me
　When the Great Juggler I must face.

VIII

We two were married, due and legal :
　Honest we've lived since we've been one.
Lord ! I could then jump like an eagle :
　You danced bright as a bit o' the sun.
Birds in a May-bush we were ! right merry !
　All night we kiss'd, we juggled all day.
Joy was the heart of Juggling Jerry !
　Now from his old girl he's juggled away.

IX

It's past parsons to console us :
　No, nor no doctor fetch for me :
I can die without my bolus ;
　Two of a trade, lass, never agree !
Parson and Doctor !—don't they love rarely,
　Fighting the devil in other men's fields !
Stand up yourself and match him fairly :
　Then see how the rascal yields !

X

I, lass, have lived no gipsy, flaunting
　　Finery while his poor helpmate grubs:
Coin I 've stored, and you won't be wanting:
　　You shan't beg from the troughs and tubs.
Nobly you 've stuck to me, though in his kitchen
　　Many a Marquis would hail you Cook!
Palaces you could have ruled and grown rich in,
　　But your old Jerry you never forsook.

IX

Hand up the chirper! ripe ale winks in it;
　　Let 's have comfort and be at peace.
Once a stout draught made me light as a linnet.
　　Cheer up! the Lord must have his lease.
May be—for none see in that black hollow—
　　It 's just a place where we 're held in pawn,
And, when the Great Juggler makes as to
　　　swallow,
It 's just the sword-trick—I ain't quite gone!

XII

Yonder came smells of the gorse, so nutty,
　　Gold-like and warm: it 's the prime of May.

Better than mortar, brick and putty,
  Is God's house on a blowing day.
Lean me more up the mound ; now I feel it :
  All the old heath-smells !   Ain't it strange ?
There 's the world laughing, as if to conceal it,
  But He 's by us, juggling the change.

XIII

I mind it well, by the sea-beach lying,
  Once—it 's long gone—when two gulls we
    beheld,
Which, as the moon got up, were flying
  Down a big wave that sparked and swelled.
Crack, went a gun : one fell : the second
  Wheeled round him twice, and was off for new
    luck :
There in the dark her white wing beckon'd :—
  Drop me a kiss—I 'm the bird dead-struck !

THE OLD CHARTIST

I

WHATE'ER I be, old England is my dam!
    So there's my answer to the judges, clear.
I'm nothing of a fox, nor of a lamb;
    I don't know how to bleat nor how to leer:
        I'm for the nation!
    That's why you see me by the wayside here,
      Returning home from transportation.

II

It's Summer in her bath this morn, I think.
    I'm fresh as dew, and chirpy as the birds:
And just for joy to see old England wink
    Thro' leaves again, I could harangue the herds:
        Isn't it something
    To speak out like a man when you've got words,
      And prove you're not a stupid dumb thing?
194

III

They shipp'd me off for it; I'm here again.
 Old England is my dam, whate'er I be!
Says I, I'll tramp it home, and see the grain:
 If you see well, you're king of what you see:
    Eyesight is having,
 If you're not given, I said, to gluttony.
  Such talk to ignorance sounds as raving.

IV

You dear old brook, that from his Grace's park
 Come bounding! on you run near my old town:
My lord can't lock the water; nor the lark,
 Unless he kills him, can my lord keep down.
    Up, is the song-note!
I've tried it, too:—for comfort and renown,
 I rather pitch'd upon the wrong note.

V

I'm not ashamed: Not beaten's still my boast:
 Again I'll rouse the people up to strike.

But home's where different politics jar most.
   Respectability the women like.
         This form, or that form,—
   The Government may be hungry pike,
     But don't you mount a Chartist platform !

VI

Well, well !   Not beaten—spite of them, I shout
   And my estate is suffering for the Cause.—
No,—what is yon brown water-rat about,
   Who washes his old poll with busy paws ?
         What does he mean by 't ?
It's like defying all our natural laws,
     For him to hope that he 'll get clean by 't.

VII

His seat is on a mud-bank, and his trade
   Is dirt :—he 's quite contemptible ; and yet
The fellow 's all as anxious as a maid
   To show a decent dress, and dry the wet.
         Now it 's his whisker,
And now his nose, and ear : he seems to get
     Each moment at the motion brisker !

VIII

To see him squat like little chaps at school,
  I could let fly a laugh with all my might.
He peers, hangs both his fore-paws:—bless that
    fool,
  He's bobbing at his frill now!—what a sight!
    Licking the dish up,
  As if he thought to pass from black to white,
    Like parson into lawny bishop.

IX

The elms and yellow reed-flags in the sun,
  Look on quite grave:—the sunlight flecks his
    side;
And links of bindweed-flowers round him run,
  And shine up doubled with him in the tide.
    I'm nearly splitting,
  But nature seems like seconding his pride,
    And thinks that his behaviour's fitting.

X

That isle o' mud looks baking dry with gold.
  His needle-muzzle still works out and in.

It really is a wonder to behold,
   And makes me feel the bristles of my chin.
      Judged by appearance,
   I fancy of the two I'm nearer Sin,
     And might as well commence a clearance.

XI

And   that's   what   my   fine   daughter   said:—she
     meant:
Pray, hold your tongue, and wear a Sunday face.
Her husband, the young linendraper, spent
   Much argument thereon :—I'm their disgrace.
      Bother the couple !
I feel superior to a chap whose place
   Commands him to be neat and supple.

XII

But if I go and say to my old hen :
   I'll mend the gentry's boots, and keep discreet,
Until they grow *too* violent,—why, then,
   A warmer welcome I might chance to meet:
      Warmer and better.
And if she fancies her old cock is beat,
   And drops upon her knees—so let her !

XIII

She suffered for me :—women, you 'll observe,
  Don't suffer for a Cause, but for a man.
When I was in the dock she show'd her nerve :
  I saw beneath her shawl my old tea-can
      Trembling . . . she brought it
  To screw me for my work : she loath'd my plan,
    And therefore doubly kind I thought it.

XIV

I 've never lost the taste of that same tea :
  That liquor on my logic floats like oil,
When I state facts, and fellows disagree.
  For human creatures all are in a coil ;
      All may want pardon.
  I see a day when every pot will boil
    Harmonious in one great Tea-garden !

XV

We wait the setting of the Dandy's day,
  Before that time !—He 's furbishing his dress,—
He *will* be ready for it !—and I say,
  That yon old dandy rat amid the cress,—
      Thanks to hard labour !—

If cleanliness is next to godliness,
   The old fat fellow's heaven's neighbour!

XVI

You teach me a fine lesson, my old boy!
   I've looked on my superiors far too long,
And small has been my profit as my joy.
   You've done the right while I've denounced
      the wrong.
         Prosper me later!
Like you I will despise the sniggering throng,
   And please myself and my Creator.

XVII

I'll bring the linendraper and his wife
   Some day to see you; taking off my hat.
Should they ask why, I'll answer: in my life
   I never found so true a democrat.
        Base occupation
Can't rob you of your own esteem, old rat!
   I'll preach you to the British nation.

MARTIN'S PUZZLE

I

THERE she goes up the street with her book in her
    hand,
  And her Good morning, Martin! Ay, lass, how
    d' ye do?
Very well, thank you, Martin!—I can't understand!
  I might just as well never have cobbled a shoe!
I can't understand it. She talks like a song;
  Her voice takes your ear like the ring of a glass;
She seems to give gladness while limping along,
  Yet sinner ne'er suffer'd like that little lass.

II

First, a fool of a boy ran her down with a cart.
  Then, her fool of a father—a blacksmith by trade—
Why the deuce does he tell us it half broke his
    heart?
  His heart!—where's the leg of the poor little
    maid!

Well, that's not enough; they must push her
    downstairs,
    To make her go crooked: but why count the
        list?
If it's right to suppose that our human affairs
    Are all order'd by heaven—there, bang goes my
        fist!

III

For if angels can look on such sights—never mind!
    When you're next to blaspheming, it's best to be
        mum.
The parson declares that her woes weren't designed;
    But, then, with the parson it's all kingdom-come.
Lose a leg, save a soul—a convenient text;
    I call it Tea doctrine, not savouring of God.
When poor little Molly wants 'chastening,' why, next
    The Archangel Michael might taste of the rod.

IV

But, to see the poor darling go limping for miles
    To read books to sick people!—and just of an age
When girls learn the meaning of ribands and smiles!
    Makes me feel like a squirrel that turns in a cage.

The more I push thinking the more I revolve :
  I never get farther :—and as to her face,
It starts up when near on my puzzle I solve,
    And says, 'This crush'd body seems such a sad
    case.'

V

Not that she's for complaining : she reads to earn
    pence ;
  And from those who can't pay, simple thanks are
    enough.
Does she leave lamentation for chaps without sense ?
  Howsoever, she's made up of wonderful stuff.
Ay, the soul in her body must be a stout cord ;
  She sings little hymns at the close of the day,
Though she has but three fingers to lift to the Lord,
  And only one leg to kneel down with to pray.

VI

What I ask is, Why persecute such a poor dear,
  If there's Law above all ? Answer that if you can!
Irreligious I'm not ; but I look on this sphere
  As a place where a man should just think like a
  man.

It isn't fair dealing!   But, contrariwise,
  Do bullets in battle the wicked select?
Why, then it's all chance-work!   And yet, in her
    eyes,
  She holds a fixed something by which I am
    checked.

VII

Yonder riband of sunshine aslope on the wall,
  If you eye it a minute 'll have the same look:
So kind! and so merciful!   God of us all!
  It's the very same lesson we get from the
    Book.
Then, is Life but a trial?   Is that what is meant?
  Some must toil, and some perish, for others
    below:
The injustice to each spreads a common content;
  Ay! I've lost it again, for it can't be quite so.

VIII

She's the victim of fools: that seems nearer the
  mark.
  On earth there are engines and numerous fools.

Why the Lord can permit them, we're still in the
    dark ;
  He does, and in some sort of way they're His
    tools.
It's a roundabout way, with respect let me add,
  If Molly goes crippled that we may be taught :
But, perhaps, it's the only way, though it's so
    bad ;
  In that case we'll bow down our heads,—as we
    ought.

IX

But the worst of *me* is, that when I bow my
    head,
  I perceive a thought wriggling away in the
    dust,
And I follow its tracks, quite forgetful, instead
  Of humble acceptance : for, question I must !
Here's a creature made carefully—carefully made !
  Put together with craft, and then stamped on,
    and why ?
The answer seems nowhere : it's discord that's
    played.
  The sky's a blue dish !—an implacable sky !

X

Stop a moment.   I seize an idea from the pit.
　They tell us that discord, though discord, alone,
Can be harmony when the notes properly fit:
　Am I judging all things from a single false tone?
Is the Universe one immense Organ, that rolls
　From devils to angels? I'm blind with the sight.
It pours such a splendour on heaps of poor souls!
　I might try at kneeling with Molly to-night.

A BALLAD OF FAIR LADIES IN REVOLT

I

SEE the sweet women, friend, that lean beneath
The ever-falling fountain of green leaves
Round the white bending stem, and like a wreath
Of our most blushful flower shine trembling
    through,
To teach philosophers the thirst of thieves:
    Is one for me? is one for you?

II

—Fair sirs, we give you welcome, yield you place,
And you shall choose among us which you will,
Without the idle pastime of the chase,
If to this treaty you can well agree:
To wed our cause, and its high task fulfil.
    He who's for us, for him are we!

III

—Most gracious ladies, nigh when light has birth,
A troop of maids, brown as burnt heather-bells,
And rich with life as moss-roots breathe of earth
In the first plucking of them, past us flew
To labour, singing rustic ritornells:
  Had they a cause? are they of you?

IV

—Sirs, they are as unthinking armies are
To thoughtful leaders, and our cause is theirs.
When they know men they know the state of war:
But now they dream like sunlight on a sea,
And deem you hold the half of happy pairs.
  He who's for us, for him are we!

V

—Ladies, I listened to a ring of dames;
Judicial in the robe and wig; secure
As venerated portraits in their frames;
And they denounced some insurrection new
Against sound laws which keep you good and
    pure.
  Are you of them? are they of you?

VI

—Sirs, they are of us, as their dress denotes,
    And by as much : let them together chime :
    It is an ancient bell within their throats,
    Pulled by an aged ringer; with what glee
    Befits the yellow yesterdays of time.
            He who's for us, for him are we !

VII

—Sweet ladies, you with beauty, you with wit;
    Dowered of all favours and all blessed things
    Whereat the ruddy torch of Love is lit;
    Wherefore this vain and outworn strife renew,
    Which stays the tide no more than eddy-rings?
            Who is for love must be for you.

VIII

—The manners of the market, honest sirs,
    'Tis hard to quit when you behold the wares.
    You flatter us, or perchance our milliners
    You flatter; so this vain and outworn She
    May still be the charmed snake to your soft airs !
            A higher lord than Love claim we.

o

IX

—One day, dear lady, missing the broad track,
I came on a wood's border, by a mead,
Where golden May ran up to moted black:
And there I saw Queen Beauty hold review,
With Love before her throne in act to plead
    Take him for me, take her for you.

X

—Ingenious gentleman, the tale is known.
Love pleaded sweetly: Beauty would not melt:
She would not melt: he turned in wrath: her
    throne
The shadow of his back froze witheringly,
And sobbing at his feet Queen Beauty knelt.
    O not such slaves of Love are we !

XI

—Love, lady, like the star above that lance
Of radiance flung by sunset on ridged cloud,
Sad as the last line of a brave romance!—
Young Love hung dim, yet quivering round him
    threw

Beams of fresh fire, while Beauty waned and
  bowed.
    Scorn Love, and dread the doom for you.

XII

—Called she not for her mirror, sir ?   Forth ran
Her women : I am lost, she cried, when lo,
Love in the form of an admiring man
Once more in adoration bent the knee,
And brought the faded Pagan to full blow :
    For which her throne she gave : not we !

XIII

—My version, madam, runs not to that end.
A certain madness of an hour half past,
Caught her like fever ; her just lord no friend
She fancied ; aimed beyond beauty, and thence
  grew
The prim acerbity, sweet Love's outcast.
    Great heaven ward off that stroke from you !

XIV

—Your prayer to heaven, good sir, is generous :
How generous likewise that you do not name

Offended nature ! She from all of us
Couched idle underneath our showering tree,
May quite withhold her most destructive flame ;
    And then what woeful women we !

xv

—Quite, could not be, fair lady ; yet your youth
May run to drought in visionary schemes :
And a late waking to perceive the truth,
When day falls shrouding her supreme adieu,
Shows darker wastes than unaccomplished dreams :
    And that may be in store for you.

xvi

—O sir, the truth, the truth ! is 't in the skies,
Or in the grass, or in this heart of ours ?
But O the truth, the truth ! the many eyes
That look on it ! the diverse things they see,
According to their thirst for fruit or flowers !
    Pass on : it is the truth seek we.

xvii

—Lady, there is a truth of settled laws
That down the past burns like a great watch-fire.

Let youth hail changeful mornings ; but your
    cause,
Whetting its edge to cut the race in two,
Is felony : you forfeit the bright lyre,
      Much honour and much glory you !

XVIII

—Sir, was it glory, was it honour, pride,
    And not as cat and serpent and poor slave,
Wherewith we walked in union by your side ?
Spare to false womanliness her delicacy,
Or bid true manliness give ear, we crave :
      In our defence thus chained are we.

XIX

—Yours, madam, were the privileges of life
    Proper to man's ideal ; you were the mark
Of action, and the banner in the strife :
Yea, of your very weakness once you drew
The strength that sounds the wells, outflies the
    lark :
      Wrapped in a robe of flame were you !

XX

—Your friend looks thoughtful.   Sir, when we
      were chill,
  You clothed us warmly; all in honour! when
  We starved you fed us; all in honour still:
  Oh, all in honour, ultra-honourably!
  Deep is the gratitude we owe to men,
            For privileged indeed were we!

XXI

—You cite exceptions, madam, that are sad,
  But come in the red struggle of our growth.
  Alas, that I should have to say it! bad
  Is two-sexed upon earth: this which you do,
  Shows animal impatience, mental sloth:
            Man monstrous! pining seraphs you!

XXII

—I fain would ask your friend . . . but I will ask
  You, sir, how if in place of numbers vague,
  Your sad exceptions were to break that mask
  They wear for your cool mind historically,
  And blaze like black lists of a *present* plague?
            But in that light behold them we.

XXIII

—Your spirit breathes a mist upon our world,
Lady, and like a rain to pierce the roof
And drench the bed where toil-tossed man lies
    curled
In his hard-earned oblivion ! You are few,
Scattered, ill-counselled, blinded : for a proof,
      I have lived, and have known none like you.

XXIV

—We may be blind to men, sir: we embrace
A future now beyond the fowler's nets.
Though few, we hold a promise for the race
That was not at our rising : you are free
To win brave mates ; you lose but marionnettes.
      He who's for us, for him are we.

XXV

—Ah ! madam, were they puppets who withstood
Youth's cravings for adventure to preserve
The dedicated ways of womanhood ?
The light which leads us from the paths of rue,
That light above us, never seen to swerve,
      Should be the home-lamp trimmed by you.

XXVI

—Ah ! sir, our worshipped posture we perchance
  Shall not abandon, though we see not how,
  Being to that lamp-post fixed, we may advance
  Beside our lords in any real degree,
  Unless we move : and to advance is now
      A sovereign need, think more than we.

XXVII

—So push you out of harbour in small craft,
  With little seamanship ; and comes a gale,
  The world will laugh, the world has often laughed,
  Lady, to see how bold when skies are blue,
  When black winds churn the deeps how panic-pale,
      How swift to the old nest fly you !

XXVIII

—What thinks your friend, kind sir ? We have
      escaped
  But partly that old half-tamed wild beast's paw
  Whereunder woman, the weak thing, was shaped:
  Men, too, have known the cramping enemy

In grim brute force, whom force of brain shall
   awe :
      Him our deliverer, await we !

XXIX

—Delusions are with eloquence endowed,
   And yours might pluck an angel from the spheres
   To play in this revolt whereto you are vowed,
   Deliverer, lady ! but like summer dew
   O'er fields that crack for rain your friends drop
      tears,
         Who see the awakening for you.

XXX

—Is he our friend, there silent ? he weeps not.
   O sir, delusion mounting like a sun
   On a mind blank as the white wife of Lot,
   Giving it warmth and movement ! if this be
   Delusion, think of what thereby was won
         For men, and dream of what win we.

XXXI

—Lady, the destiny of minor powers,
   Who would recast us, is but to convulse :

You enter on a strife that frets and sours;
You can but win sick disappointment's hue;
And simply an accelerated pulse,
    Some tonic you have drunk moves you.

XXXII

—Thinks your friend so? Good sir, your wit is
    bright;
But wit that strives to speak the popular voice,
Puts on its nightcap and puts out its light.
Curfew, would seem your conqueror's decree
To women likewise: and we have no choice
    Save darkness or rebellion, we!

XXXIII

—A plain safe intermediate way is cleft
By reason foiling passion: you that rave
Of mad alternatives to right and left
Echo the tempter, madam: and 'tis due
Unto your sex to shun it as the grave,
    This later apple offered you.

XXXIV

—This apple is not ripe, it is not sweet;
  Nor rosy, sir, nor golden : eye and mouth
  Are little wooed by it ; yet we would eat.
  We are somewhat tired of Eden, is our plea.
  We have thirsted long; this apple suits our drouth:
      'Tis good for men to halve, think we.

XXXV

—But say, what seek you, madam ?   'Tis enough
  That you should have dominion o'er the springs
  Domestic and man's heart: those ways, how rough,
  How vile, outside the stately avenue
  Where you walk sheltered by your angel's wings,
      Are happily unknown to you.

XXXVI

—We hear women's shrieks on them. We like
      your phrase,
  Dominion domestic !   And that roar,
  'What seek you ?' is of tyrants in all days.
  Sir, get you something of our purity

And we will of your strength : we ask no more.
   That is the sum of what seek we.

XXXVII

—O for an image, madam, in one word,
   To show you as the lightning night reveals,
   Your error and your perils : you have erred
   In mind only, and the perils that ensue
   Swift heels may soften ; wherefore to swift heels
      Address your hopes of safety you !

XXXVIII

—To err in mind, sir . . . your friend smiles : he
     may !
   To err in mind, if err in mind we can,
   Is grievous error you do well to stay.
   But O how different from reality
   Men's fiction is ! how like you in the plan,
      Is woman, knew you her as we !

XXXIX

—Look, lady, where yon river winds its line
   Toward sunset, and receives on breast and face

The splendour of fair life : to be divine,
'Tis nature bids you be to nature true,
Flowing with beauty, lending earth your grace,
    Reflecting heaven in clearness you.

XL

—Sir, you speak well : your friend no word vouch-
    safes.
To flow with beauty, breeding fools and worse,
Cowards and worse : at such fair life she chafes,
Who is not wholly of the nursery,
Nor of your schools : we share the primal curse ;
    Together shake it off, say we !

XLI

—Hear, then, my friend, madam ! Tongue-restrained
    he stands
Till words are thoughts, and thoughts, like swords
    enriched
With traceries of the artificer's hands,
Are fire-proved steel to cut, fair flowers to view.—
Do I hear him ?   Oh, he is bewitched, bewitched !
    Heed him not !   Traitress beauties you !

XLII

—We have won a champion, sisters, and a sage!

—Ladies, you win a guest to a good feast!

—Sir spokesman, sneers are weakness veiling rage.

—Of weakness, and wise men, you have the key.

—Then are there fresher mornings mounting East

      Than ever yet have dawned, sing we!

XLIII

—False ends as false began, madam, be sure!

—What lure there is the pure cause purifies!

—Who purifies the victim of the lure?

—That soul which bids us our high light pursue.

—Some heights are measured down: the wary wise

      Shun Reason in the masque with you!

XLIV

—Sir, for the friend you bring us, take our thanks.

  Yes, Beauty was of old this barren goal;

  A thing with claws; and brute-like in her
      pranks!

  But could she give more loyal guarantee

  Than wooing Wisdom, that in her a soul

      Has risen?   Adieu: content are we!

XLV

Those ladies led their captive to the flood's
Green edge. He floating with them seemed the
  most
Fool-flushed old noddy ever crowned with buds.
Happier than I ! Then, why not wiser too ?
For he that lives with Beauty, he may boast
  His comrade over me and you.

XLVI

Have women nursed some dream since Helen sailed
Over the sea of blood the blushing star,
That beauty, whom frail man as Goddess hailed,
When not possessing her (for such is he !),
Might in a wondering season seen afar,
  Be tamed to say not ' I,' but ' we ' ?

XLVII

And shall they make of Beauty their estate,
The fortress and the weapon of their sex ?
Shall she in her frost-brilliancy dictate,
More queenly than of old, how we must woo,
Ere she will melt ? The halter 's on our necks,
  Kick as it likes us, I and you.

XLVIII

Certain it is, if Beauty has disdained
Her ancient conquests, with an aim thus high
If this, if that, if more, the fight is gained.
But can she keep her followers without fee?
Yet ah! to hear anew those ladies cry,
   He who's for us, for him are we

THE WOODS OF WESTERMAIN

I

ENTER these enchanted woods,
   You who dare.
Nothing harms beneath the leaves
More than waves a swimmer cleaves.
Toss your heart up with the lark,
Foot at peace with mouse and worm,
   Fair you fare.
Only at a dread of dark
Quaver, and they quit their form:
Thousand eyeballs under hoods
   Have you by the hair.
Enter these enchanted woods,
   You who dare.

P

II

Here the snake across your path
Stretches in his golden bath:
Mossy-footed squirrels leap
Soft as winnowing plumes of Sleep:
Yaffles on a chuckle skim
Low to laugh from branches dim:
Up the pine, where sits the star,
Rattles deep the moth-winged jar.
Each has business of his own;
But should you distrust a tone,
    Then beware.
Shudder all the haunted roods,
All the eyeballs under hoods
    Shroud you in their glare.
Enter these enchanted woods,
    You who dare.

III

Open hither, open hence.
Scarce a bramble weaves a fence,
Where the strawberry runs red,
With white star-flower overhead;

Cumbered by dry twig and cone,
Shredded husks of seedlings flown,
Mine of mole and spotted flint:
Of dire wizardry no hint,
Save mayhap the print that shows
Hasty outward-tripping toes,
Heels to terror on the mould.
These, the woods of Westermain,
Are as others to behold,
Rich of wreathing sun and rain;
Foliage lustreful around
Shadowed leagues of slumbering sound.
Wavy tree-tops, yellow whins,
Shelter eager minikins,
Myriads, free to peck and pipe:
Would you better? would you worse?
You with them may gather ripe
Pleasures flowing not from purse.
Quick and far as Colour flies
Taking the delighted eyes,
You of any well that springs
May unfold the heaven of things;
Have it homely and within,
And thereof its likeness win,

Will you so in soul's desire :
This do sages grant t' the lyre.
This is being bird and more,
More than glad musician this ;
Granaries you will have a store
Past the world of woe and bliss ;
Sharing still its bliss and woe ;
Harnessed to its hungers, no.
On the throne Success usurps,
You shall seat the joy you feel
Where a race of water chirps,
Twisting hues of flourished steel :
Or where light is caught in hoop
Up a clearing's leafy rise,
Where the crossing deerherds troop
Classic splendours, knightly dyes.
Or, where old-eyed oxen chew
Speculation with the cud,
Read their pool of vision through,
Back to hours when mind was mud ;
Nigh the knot, which did untwine
Timelessly to drowsy suns ;
Seeing Earth a slimy spine,
Heaven a space for winging tons.

Farther, deeper, may you read,
Have you sight for things afield,
Where peeps she, the Nurse of seed,
Cloaked, but in the peep revealed;
Showing a kind face and sweet:
Look you with the soul you see 't.
Glory narrowing to grace,
Grace to glory magnified,
Following that will you embrace
Close in arms or aëry wide.
Banished is the white Foam-born
Not from here, nor under ban
Phoebus lyrist, Phoebe's horn,
Pipings of the reedy Pan.
Loved of Earth of old they were,
Loving did interpret her;
And the sterner worship bars
None whom Song has made her stars.
You have seen the huntress moon
Radiantly facing dawn,
Dusky meads between them strewn
Glimmering like downy awn:
Argent Westward glows the hunt,
East the blush about to climb;

One another fair they front,
Transient, yet outshine the time;
Even as dewlight off the rose
In the mind a jewel sows.
Thus opposing grandeurs live
Here if Beauty be their dower:
Doth she of her spirit give,
Fleetingness will spare her flower.
This is in the tune we play,
Which no spring of strength would quell;
In subduing does not slay;
Guides the channel, guards the well:
Tempered holds the young blood-heat,
Yet through measured grave accord,
Hears the heart of wildness beat
Like a centaur's hoof on sward.
Drink the sense the notes infuse,
You a larger self will find:
Sweetest fellowship ensues
With the creatures of your kind.
Ay, and Love, if Love it be
Flaming over *I* and *ME*,
Love meet they who do not shove
Cravings in the van of Love.

Courtly dames are here to woo,
Knowing love if it be true.
Reverence the blossom-shoot
Fervently, they are the fruit.
Mark them stepping, hear them talk,
Goddess, is no myth inane,
You will say of those who walk
In the woods of Westermain.
Waters that from throat and thigh
Dart the sun his arrows back;
Leaves that on a woodland sigh
Chat of secret things no lack;
Shadowy branch-leaves, waters clear,
Bare or veiled they move sincere;
Not by slavish terrors tripped
Being anew in nature dipped,
Growths of what they step on, these;
With the roots the grace of trees.
Casket-breasts they give, nor hide,
For a tyrant's flattered pride,
Mind, which nourished not by light;
Lurks the shuffling trickster sprite:
Whereof are strange tales to tell;
Some in blood writ, tombed in bell.

Here the ancient battle ends,
Joining two astonished friends,
Who the kiss can give and take
With more warmth than in that world
Where the tiger claws the snake,
Snake her tiger clasps infurled,
And the issue of their fight
People lands in snarling plight.
Here her splendid beast she leads
Silken-leashed and decked with weeds
Wild as he, but breathing faint
Sweetness of unfelt constraint.
Love, the great volcano, flings
Fires of lower Earth to sky;
Love, the sole permitted, sings
Sovereignly of *ME* and *I.*
Bowers he has of sacred shade,
Spaces of superb parade,
Voiceful . . . But bring you a note
Wrangling, howsoe'er remote,
Discords out of discord spin
Round and round derisive din :
Sudden will a pallor pant
Chill at screeches miscreant;

Owls or spectres, thick they flee;
Nightmare upon horror broods;
Hooded laughter, monkish glee,
    Gaps the vital air.
Enter these enchanted woods
    You who dare.

IV

You must love the light so well
That no darkness will seem fell.
Love it so you could accost
Fellowly a livid ghost.
Whish! the phantom wisps away,
Owns him smoke to cocks of day.
In your breast the light must burn
Fed of you, like corn in quern
Ever plumping while the wheel
Speeds the mill and drains the meal.
Light to light sees little strange,
Only features heavenly new;
Then you touch the nerve of Change,
Then of Earth you have the clue;
Then her two-sexed meanings melt
Through you, wed the thought and felt.

Sameness locks no scurfy pond
Here for Custom, crazy-fond :
Change is on the wing to bud
Rose in brain from rose in blood.
Wisdom throbbing shall you see
Central in complexity ;
From her pasture 'mid the beasts
Rise to her ethereal feasts,
Not, though lightnings track your wit
Starward, scorning them you quit :
For be sure the bravest wing
Preens it in our common spring,
Thence along the vault to soar,
You with others, gathering more,
Glad of more, till you reject
Your proud title of elect,
Perilous even here while few
Roam the arched greenwood with you.
      Heed that snare.
Muffled by his cavern-cowl
Squats the scaly Dragon-fowl,
Who was lord ere light you drank,
And lest blood of knightly rank
Stream, let not your fair princess

Stray: he holds the leagues in stress,
　　Watches keenly there.
Oft has he been riven; slain
Is no force in Westermain.
Wait, and we shall forge him curbs,
Put his fangs to uses, tame,
Teach him, quick as cunning herbs,
How to cure him sick and lame.
Much restricted, much enringed,
Much he frets, the hooked and winged,
　　Never known to spare.
'Tis enough: the name of Sage
Hits no thing in nature, nought;
Man the least, save when grave Age
From yon Dragon guards his thought.
Eye him when you hearken dumb
To what words from Wisdom come.
When she says how few are by
Listening to her, eye his eye.
　　Self, his name declare.
Him shall Change, transforming late,
Wonderously renovate.
Hug himself the creature may:
What he hugs is loathed decay.

Crying, slip thy scales, and slough !
Change will strip his armour off;
Make of him who was all maw,
Inly only thrilling-shrewd,
Such a servant as none saw
Through his days of dragonhood.
Days when growling o'er his bone,
Sharpened he for mine and thine;
Sensitive within alone;
Scaly as the bark of pine.
Change, the strongest son of Life,
Has the Spirit here to wife.
Lo, their young of vivid breed,
Bear the lights that onward speed,
Threading thickets, mounting glades,
Up the verdurous colonnades,
Round the fluttered curves, and down,
Out of sight of Earth's blue crown,
Whither, in her central space,
Spouts the Fount and Lure o' the chase.
Fount unresting, Lure divine !
There meet all: too late look most.
Fire in water hued as wine,
Springs amid a shadowy host,

Circled : one close-headed mob,
Breathless, scanning divers heaps,
Where a Heart begins to throb,
Where it ceases, slow, with leaps.
And 'tis very strange, 'tis said,
How you spy in each of them
Semblance of that Dragon red,
As the oak in bracken-stem.
And, 'tis said, how each and each :
Which commences, which subsides :
First my Dragon ! doth beseech
Her who food for all provides.
And she answers with no sign ,
Utters neither yea nor nay ;
Fires the water hued as wine ;
Kneads another spark in clay.
Terror is about her hid ;
Silence of the thunders locked ;
Lightnings lining the shut lid ;
Fixity on quaking rocked.
Lo, you look at Flow and Drought
Interflashed and interwrought :
Ended is begun, begun
Ended, quick as torrents run.

Young Impulsion spouts to sink ;
Luridness and lustre link ;
'Tis your come and go of breath ;
Mirrored pants the Life, the Death ;
Each of either reaped and sown :
Rosiest rosy wanes to crone.
See you so ? your senses drift ;
'Tis a shuttle weaving swift.
Look with spirit past the sense,
Spirit shines in permanence.
That is She, the view of whom
Is the dust within the tomb,
Is the inner blush above,
Look to loathe, or look to love ;
Think her Lump, or know her Flame ;
Dread her scourge, or read her aim ;
Shoot your hungers from their nerve ;
Or, in her example, serve.
Some have found her sitting grave ;
Laughing, some ; or, browed with sweat,
Hurling dust of fool and knave
In a hissing smithy's jet.
More it were not well to speak ;
Burn to see, you need but seek.

Once beheld she gives the key
Airing every doorway, she.
Little can you stop or steer
Ere of her you are the seër.
On the surface she will witch,
Rendering Beauty yours, but gaze
Under, and the soul is rich
Past computing, past amaze.
Then is courage that endures
Even her awful tremble yours.
Then, the reflex of that Fount
Spied below, will Reason mount
Lordly and a quenchless force,
Lighting Pain to its mad source,
Scaring Fear till Fear escapes,
Shot through all its phantom shapes.
Then your spirit will perceive
Fleshly seed of fleshly sins ;
Where the passions interweave,
How the serpent tangle spins
Of the sense of Earth misprised,
Brainlessly unrecognized ;
She being Spirit in her clods,
Footway to the God of Gods.

Then for you are pleasures pure,
Sureties as the stars are sure:
Not the wanton beckoning flags
Which, of flattery and delight,
Wax to the grim Habit-Hags
Riding souls of men to night:
Pleasures that through blood run sane,
Quickening spirit from the brain.
Each of each in sequent birth,
Blood and brain and spirit, three
(Say the deepest gnomes of Earth),
Join for true felicity.
Are they parted, then expect
Some one sailing will be wrecked:
Separate hunting are they sped,
Scan the morsel coveted.
Earth that Triad is: she hides
Joy from him who that divides;
Showers it when the three are one
Glassing her in union.
Earth your haven, Earth your helm,
You command a double realm,
Labouring here to pay your debt,
Till your little sun shall set;

Leaving her the future task:
Loving her too well to ask.
Eglantine that climbs the yew,
She her darkest wreathes for those
Knowing her the Ever-new,
And themselves the kin o' the rose.
Life, the chisel, axe and sword,
Wield who have her depths explored:
Life, the dream, shall be their robe
Large as air about the globe;
Life, the question, hear its cry
Echoed with concordant Why;
Life, the small self-dragon ramped,
Thrill for service to be stamped.
Ay, and over every height
Life for them shall wave a wand:
That, the last, where sits affright,
Homely shows the stream beyond.
Love the light and be its lynx,
You will track her and attain;
Read her as no cruel Sphinx
In the woods of Westermain.
Daily fresh the woods are ranged;
Glooms which otherwhere appal,

Q

Sounded : here, their worths exchanged
Urban joins with pastoral :
Little lost, save what may drop
Husk-like, and the mind preserves.
Natural overgrowths they lop,
Yet from nature neither swerves,
Trained or savage : for this cause :
Of our Earth they ply the laws,
Have in Earth their feeding root,
Mind of man and bent of brute.
Hear that song ; both wild and ruled.
Hear it : is it wail or mirth ?
Ordered, bubbled, quite unschooled ?
None, and all : it springs of Earth.
O but hear it ! 'tis the mind ;
Mind that with deep Earth unites,
Round the solid trunk to wind
Rings of clasping parasites.
Music have you there to feed
Simplest and most soaring need.
Free to wind, and in desire
Winding, they to her attached
Feel the trunk a spring of fire,
And ascend to heights unmatched,

Whence the tidal world is viewed
As a sea of windy wheat,
Momently black, barren, rude ;
Golden-brown, for harvest meet,
Dragon-reaped from folly-sown ;
Bride-like to the sickle-blade :
Quick it varies, while the moan,
Moan of a sad creature strayed,
Chiefly is its voice.   So flesh
Conjures tempest-flails to thresh
Good from worthless.   Some clear lamps
Light it ; more of dead marsh-damps.
Monster is it still, and blind,
Fit but to be led by Pain.
Glance we at the paths behind,
Fruitful sight has Westermain.
There we laboured, and in turn
Forward our blown lamps discern,
As you see on the dark deep
Far the loftier billows leap,
　　　Foam for beacon bear.
Hither, hither, if you will,
Drink instruction, or instil,
Run the woods like vernal sap,

Crying, hail to luminousness!
　　But have care.
In yourself may lurk the trap:
On conditions they caress.
Here you meet the light invoked
Here is never secret cloaked.
Doubt you with the monster's fry
All his orbit may exclude;
Are you of the stiff, the dry,
Cursing the not understood;
Grasp you with the monster's claws;
Govern with his truncheon-saws;
Hate, the shadow of a grain;
You are lost in Westermain:
Earthward swoops a vulture sun,
Nighted upon carrion:
Straightway venom wine-cups shout
Toasts to One whose eyes are out:
Flowers along the reeling floor
Drip henbane and hellebore:
Beauty, of her tresses shorn,
Shrieks as nature's maniac:
Hideousness on hoof and horn
Tumbles, yapping in her track:

Haggard Wisdom, stately once,
Leers fantastical and trips:
Allegory drums the sconce,
Impiousness nibblenips.
Imp that dances, imp that flits,
Imp o' the demon-growing girl,
Maddest! whirl with imp o' the pits
Round you, and with them you whirl
Fast where pours the fountain-rout
Out of Him whose eyes are out:
Multitudes on multitudes,
Drenched in wallowing devilry:
And you ask where you may be,
 In what reek of a lair
Given to bones and ogre-broods:
 And they yell you Where.
Enter these enchanted woods,
 You who dare.

www.ingramcontent.com/pod-product-compliance
Lightning Source LLC
Chambersburg PA
CBHW030809020726
47499CB00006B/1828